Lazarus of Bethany

A Novel

By E. Ann McIntyre

"Lazarus of Bethany"

ISBN-13 978-0-9881144-3-2
ISBN-10:0988114437

Cover Icon
Russian Icon. The Raising of Lazarus. 15th century.
The Russian Museum, St. Petersburg, Russia
Image in Public Domain

Where used Biblical Quotes are from the NIV version

Introduction

Lazarus of Bethany, Eleazar in Hebrew, is the man known as *The Friend of the Lord*. Never listed among the disciples of Jesus [Yeshua], Lazarus only appears in the Gospel According to John.

The resurrection of Lazarus by his grieving friend Jesus of Nazareth is the final miracle in John's Gospel before Jesus' passion, death, and resurrection. It is the pivotal moment in the Gospel when the temple authorities decide that Jesus must die (John 11:53) because too many people are starting to believe in him. The chief priests also plot against Lazarus (John 12:10), as his very existence testifies to the power of Jesus.

It is in John's Gospel that we learn of the identity the woman who anointed the feet of Jesus. In the Gospels of Mathew (26), Mark(14), and Luke(7) she is unnamed and has been mistaken for Mary Magdalene. In John (12) in the story of "The Anointing at Bethany" the woman is Mary [Miriam] of Bethany, the sister of Lazarus and Martha.

Outside the Gospels, there are stories that Lazarus lived in Kiton [now Laranca] Cyprus, and that he was named its first Bishop by St. Paul and St. Barnabas. The Church of St. Lazarus is there and is said to house his second grave.

Other stories have the Bethany siblings living their mission in southern France. They miraculously arrived there after a forced journey by boat. There are a number of churches built there in their honor, including another burial site for Lazarus.

The Gospel does not tell us what happened to Lazarus after Jesus brought him back to life. We have no idea how the miracle affected Lazarus. He remains a silent witness to his friend who loved him.

This story is a fictional offering about Lazarus of Bethany and his relationship with Jesus of Nazareth. It is a story about two boys who lived in an occupied state, in a troubled land and grew into manhood together.

It is a story of two men, two deaths, two resurrections, and the enemies of the truth who sought to destroy them both. It is a story of doubt, and the journey to faith, of fear, and the journey to courage, of bitterness and the journey to forgiveness.

E. Ann McIntyre

Prologue

Bethany, Israel A.D.33: One week before Passover

"Where is he? Why has he not come?" Through the fog of my overheated brain, I knew Martha was annoyed with our friend Yeshua. I wanted to call out to her and tell her I was at peace with the inevitability of my death; however, I was unable to speak. It was my time to go. The sounds of Miriam weeping and Martha's pacing grew distant, as I felt myself lifted out of my body.

The shadow of death enveloped me. I existed in what I call the State of Waiting, where I felt a comforting presence, an incredibly loving presence. I was not alone; other souls were there too. Some of the souls were, like me, at peace in this State of Waiting. Other souls were in agony; I sensed their distress.

There was nothing to see or touch. I did not have a body, so I lacked any means or physical ability to interpret my existence. There was no darkness or light, just a state of being. I was still me, Lazarus of Bethany, with my memories and knowledge of my life intact. The State of Waiting was pleasant enough, I suppose. I felt no impatience or restlessness.

As to how long I was in that state, I have no direct knowledge. I learned later that I was in the grave for four days; to me it was timeless. During my formation as a priest, Master Yosef of Arimathea taught me about the resurrection. I wondered if this was resurrection or if there is another existence yet to come.

I prayed the psalms. I recalled the words of the prophet Job, *"I know that my Redeemer lives and that in the end, he will stand upon the earth. And after my skin has been destroyed, yet in my flesh, I will see God."* It was at that moment that Yeshua's command resonated in the depths of my being.

Part 1

See How Much He Loved Him (Jn 11:36)

Lazarus of Bethany

Chapter 1 Eleazar bar Boethius

I was born in Bethany, a small village nestled among the hills east of Jerusalem. On the eighth day of my life, I entered into Abraham's covenant with God in accordance with the Law of Moses. Presented in the Temple to my Grandfather Simeon, who was the High Priest at the time, and consecrated with the dedication name Eleazar bar Boethius, I was known to most people as Lazarus.

My father Boethius was a priest. Apart from his Temple duties, my father had an excellent wine producing business, the love of which he passed on to me. My mother Ester was an outgoing person who enjoyed having a house full of family and friends whenever she could. I think her favorite pastime was making our clothes, bed coverings, and other things on her loom. When she was not cooking, you could hear the loom going back and forth with its telltale rhythm. Our clothing went right from her loom to our backs, and fine clothes they were too.

My parents chose to raise their family outside the walled city of Jerusalem. A wise decision, considering the frequent storms of protest against the Roman occupation and the ensuing violent crackdowns by the Roman army. Our life in Bethany was relatively peaceful.

While not being overly strict with us, my parents were faithful observers of the Law and customs of our

Jewish heritage. They worked diligently at passing that faithfulness on to us their children; yes, I had siblings.

I arrived three years after my older sister Martha, who was at an age when she was accustomed to being in command of the household. My arrival, as the long wanted male offspring, did not go over well with her. I spent my first tender years in my mother's protective custody. The final addition to our family was another sister, Miriam, who was born three years after me. Martha liked her better; she spent many hours being "Mother" to our youngest sibling.

Our family was descended from the priestly line of Aaron, and according to Hebrew law; no other line of the Jewish people performed the sacrifice ritual in the Temple. All my ancestors were priests, "kohein" in Hebrew, and my father expected to serve as High Priest of the Temple as had my grandfather Simeon before him. My path was clear. From the age of six, my parents immersed me in the scriptures, the Law, and the sacred history of our people. In preparation for my life as a priest, I studied for nine years at the Temple.

Although I understood the importance of studying for my future role, I would have preferred to do something else with my life. I loved tending the family vineyard, reputed to produce the best wine in Judea. Passover was an exceptionally profitable festival for our family. I took pride in my contribution to my family's business.

The vineyard grew behind our house on a gentle hill. I followed my father through the vines and watched him inspect and prune each branch as needed. He taught me that the finest wine comes from optimal grapes that grow on the best vine branches. If the whole vine did not produce the desired quality of grapes, it became firewood. Pruning was essential to producing the most famous wine in the region. As I grew older, when I was not in the Temple, I assumed more of the responsibility of caring for the vineyard.

Working in the vineyard gave me a chance to be alone, to be by myself. I would pray and sing the psalms to my heart's content. I spent days and weeks at the Temple studying about God, but out in the vineyard is where I truly felt God's presence. I never told my father how I felt. For him, a person encountered God in the Temple and nowhere else. Only the High Priest could go before the Lord in the Holy of Holies, and the year I turned twelve he became the High Priest.

***

At twelve years old, I had one year left of religious boyhood. One more year before I could join my father in the adult section of the Temple and participate in the festivals as an adult. At the age of thirteen, I would become a Son of the Commandment, an adult under the Law of Moses.

My twelfth year was an intense time for studies and preparations. I spent five and a half days each week at the Temple school. There were other boys there too. Many were studying to be rabbis or teachers. Some were there because their families sent them for discipline training. The school was quite strict in following the Letter of The Law, and our customs.

Because I was preparing to be a priest, there were many rituals and observances I was required to learn and to some degree, practice. My father had seen to it that I had the best teachers. Master Yosef of Arimathea guided my spiritual formation. He was a Pharisee, a deeply religious man who cherished the Word of God and instilled that love in his students. Master Yosef said that we must be ever watchful for the Anointed One, the Christos, the Promised One of Israel, the descendant of King David, who would sit upon the throne of David. He taught that the One, who is to come, would do so, not as a military ruler, but as a shepherd of souls.

I often tossed the two sides around in my head, debating whether the Messiah would rule as a military hero or lead as a spiritual shepherd. I wished and hoped for the military hero. I should have listened, more with my heart than with my head, to the wise words of my masters.

Chapter 2 Friendship is Born

It was Passover week, and we were preparing to go to Jerusalem to celebrate Passover together as a family when my mother suddenly became ill. She often got headaches, but this one was so severe she could not get out of bed.

Father brought the physician, who gave my mother some myrrh to ease her pain. Martha insisted on staying home to take care of her. Miriam sat near Mother's bed crying. She thought that Mother was dying. Mother tried to comfort her, assuring Miriam and the rest of us that she was not dying. Mother knew Father had to go to the Temple, and she wanted me to go with him.

Mother rallied, and Father was satisfied that she was recovering, so we made plans to head out. Since we were only two people, we needed to find another family to join up with to celebrate the Seder meal. We were fortunate there were a number of caravans passing through Bethany on their way to Jerusalem.

Bethany's town center was a hub of activity where pilgrims stopped to get water from the town well and purchase the particular food items required for the Passover Seder. The pace of buying was less frantic here than it was in Jerusalem. We had our wine stall set up near the town well, an excellent location for sales.

I made the money exchanges while my father chatted with prospective buyers and sent them my

E. Ann McIntyre

way. During a momentary lull in the activity, I had a chance to observe the people milling around the area. That is when I saw him, a boy about my age helping a woman, I supposed was his mother get a drink of water from the well.

I watched them for a while and wished I could go over and meet him. Out of the corner of my eye, I saw my father speaking with a man; the boy looked at me and we exchanged tentative waves.

My father brought the man over to our stall and introduced me to him. He was Yosef, a carpenter from Nazareth, travelling with his family. My father said that we would join with them to celebrate Passover. Yosef called to his wife and son to join us at the stall. It was the same boy.

I was the first to speak, "Shalom, my name is Lazarus. What's yours?"

"Shalom, I'm Yeshua," he said, "I'm from Nazareth. This is my first Passover in Jerusalem. I am so excited!"

"Well," I said, "You're in luck; I study at the Temple. I will be a priest there someday. I'd be happy to show you around the City and the Temple."

"That's exciting Lazarus!" Yeshua said, "I can't wait."

We turned and headed in the direction of Jerusalem when my father called out to me.

"Lazarus, I'm glad you have a new friend, but please wait for your old Abba. We need to pack up," he said shaking his finger at me.

Yeshua and I proceeded to help my father pack up the remaining flasks of wine. We had done well in the Bethany market, and we could quickly sell the rest in Jerusalem. Yosef told us that when we got to

Jerusalem, we would stay with his wife's sister Salome and her husband, Zebedee from Capernaum.

Yosef called the older family members to come with us. They had been checking out the wares at other stalls. Yeshua introduced me to his older brothers, James, Simon, and twins Yossi and Jude, and his sister Ruth.

My father was pleased that the number of people, counting us, was sufficient in number to consume the Seder meal. Tradition dictates that all the food of the feast be consumed during the meal. This was my father's first year as the High Priest and President of the highest court of Jewish law, the Sanhedrin, and he would be the one offering our group's sacrificial lamb in the Temple.

***

We began our short trek to Jerusalem before noon. We joined a steady stream of pilgrims on the road to the Holy City and to the great Temple. I had taken this journey many times in my twelve years, but there was always something special about going to the Temple surrounded by other pilgrims. We sang songs about the Exodus of our people from Egypt to the Promised Land, from slavery to freedom. Singing the Song of Moses, we swayed and danced to the rhythm, mightily punching the air as we sang of "*the horses and riders cast into the sea*".

The road from Bethany winds its way through the Mount of Olives passing below the Garden of Gethsemane. It was from this vantage point that the Walled City of Jerusalem came into clear view. Yeshua, who walked next to me, came to a complete

7

halt. I stopped and saw the look of wonder on his face.

"Magnificent, isn't it?" I said.

"Oh yes, look how the Temple dominates the entire city," he exclaimed.

The Temple's walls towered above us, as did the Roman soldiers who stared down at the steady stream of pilgrims. There seemed to be more soldiers than usual. I was reminded just how dangerous gathering in Jerusalem can be. I tried to refocus my thoughts on the great celebration of Passover that would take place over the next several days.

Entering the city through the Beautiful Gate, we made our way through the crowded narrow streets with Yosef and family in the lead. Myriam, Yeshua's mother, took him by the hand. My father had his hand on my shoulder. In crowds like this, it was not safe for two young boys like Yeshua and I to be wandering by ourselves through the streets. Our parents kept us close.

Yosef was taking us to the Zebedee house, which was not far from the Temple. Zebedee kept a house here so he could market his fish to the Roman courts and Temple officials. Yosef assured my father that the house was big enough for all of us.

As we rounded a corner, the Temple came into full view, and Yeshua stopped again. I enjoyed watching the look on his face as he took in the scope and size of the Temple. Myriam smiled at her son and hugged him close to her side. They looked at each other and laughed.

We took a left and entered a home down the street on the right-hand side. Zebedee and Salome greeted Yosef and Myriam with the kiss of peace. Yosef introduced my father, and then myself to our hosts. They were delighted that they would have a full house for The Passover Seder.

Zebedee's son James greeted Yeshua with an embrace, and Yeshua introduced him to me. James quickly led us upstairs to a big wide-open room they called the Upper Room. This is where we would celebrate the Passover Seder. It would also serve as our sleeping quarters. James led us up another flight of stairs to the roof. The view from the roof was incredible. It had an unobstructed view of the Temple, its walls turned to gold in the late afternoon sun. I looked over at Yeshua as he stood there staring at the magnificent vista, his eyes filled with emotion. I could see his lips moving silently as he prayed.

James bar Zebedee and I stood in silence, as Yeshua continued to pray. The reflective moment was broken as Yeshua's brothers stormed the rooftop. Yeshua turned around and with obvious annoyance told his siblings to be quiet.

"Why? This is not the Temple. Don't go all weird on us Yeshua," his brother James shot back.

"*Weird?*" I thought, "*What so strange about being in awe of God's Holy Temple?*" I did not know the family well yet, so I kept my thoughts to myself. I reached out and touched Yeshua's shoulder. He nodded to me and said, "Thanks."

Susanna, daughter of Zebedee and Salome, and Ruth ascended to the roof and called us to supper, interrupting the rest of the conversation. We all scrambled down the narrow staircase, jostling each other as we went. We took our places on the cushions. I deliberately chose a spot next to Yeshua. He grabbed my hand in appreciation. He wanted me to sit next to him. We had only known each other a few hours, and we were getting along splendidly.

Zebedee deferred the invocation of the Blessing to my father. The meal consisted of food that we all brought with us; smoked fish from the Sea of Galilee, and vegetables from Myriam's garden in Nazareth. I handed Yeshua one of Martha's finest biscuits. "Hmm, your sister is an excellent cook," he said adding, "Almost as good as my mother."

Leaning against the wall for support, Yeshua and I chatted all through the meal about the coming days of Passover. I shared with him my previous experience of the feast. I reiterated my promise to show him around the Temple and introduce him to my teachers. He seemed particularly pleased about meeting my teachers. The meal ended with the final blessing. I invited Yeshua to join me back up on the roof to say our evening prayer together. He responded with delight.

The two of us went up to the roof. The others did not follow. We took a couple of spots at the center of the roof and faced the Temple. We began our prayer with a few minutes of silence. Yeshua signalled to me to take the lead in the recitation of the psalms. We prayed together for about an hour, pausing now and then to observe holy silence and soak in God's presence. I felt I had found a kindred spirit in Yeshua, and I think he felt the same way about me.

Chapter 3 Storytellers

Yeshua woke me before sun-up the next morning; he wanted to go on the roof again to say our morning prayers. Not wanting to offend my new friend, although I really just wanted to roll over and go back to sleep, I got up.

Yeshua began with the Shema, "Sh'ma Yis'ra'eil Adonai Eloheinu Adonai Echad. [Hear Israel, the Lord is our God; the Lord is One.]" He took the lead reciting the psalms. He prayed so fervently and deliberately, I wondered if he should be the priest instead of me. I looked over at him as the rising sun lit his face, which seemed to glow from within. I rubbed my eyes, thinking I was dreaming.

After our prayer time, Yeshua told me that his greatest desire was to be in close communion with God all the time. Admirable, I thought but how practical was it? We had to carry on with the day-to-day activities life demanded of us.

We headed back downstairs to find some of the other members of the household had risen before the sun. Myriam and Salome had breakfast ready, and we were both hungry. We ate quickly, eager to go to the Temple for the early-morning prayer service. As we were about to bolt out the door, I heard a gruff, "Where are you two going?" It was my father.

"We are going to the Temple," I replied.

"Lazarus, you know better than to be out on the streets of Jerusalem during a festival without an adult.

Wait until Yosef, Zebedee, and I are ready to go," my father said. During Passover, the population of Jerusalem swells to almost a million people.

Yeshua and I sat back down on the meal cushions and enjoyed listening to the older folk share stories. Passover was a feast for storytelling both formal and informal. We shared the story of our people and stories about our families.

During the conversation, Yosef mentioned that he was of the House of David. In the year of the census ordered by Caesar Augustus, he had to take his whole family to Bethlehem, and that is where Yeshua was born.

"We brought him here to the Temple eight days after his birth. Simeon was the High Priest at the time," Yosef said.

My father chimed in saying, "Simeon was my father. He performed Lazarus' dedication ceremony."

"Wow," I said, "Yeshua, we have that in common." The two of us laughed. We had only known each other a day and we felt like we had known each other for years.

****

I could feel the excitement as we made the short walk to the Temple. I could not wait to show Yeshua around. We walked through the Court of the Gentiles, a large open area where a family or group like us would buy their sacrificial lamb, and change foreign money into the acceptable denomination for the Temple. It was a busy place; a steady hum of noise emanated from the thousands of people from all over the world. There were many different languages spoken. It was fun trying to figure out what people were saying.

The Roman soldiers made their presence known, breaking up scuffles and arresting determined troublemakers. There were the perennial prophets preaching in different corners of the Temple, beating their breasts, telling anyone who would listen to prepare for the coming of the Messiah.

Merchants filled the Court of the Gentiles, selling whatever wares they could. There were endless numbers of sheepfolds from which people selected their Paschal lamb.

Our three families pooled our resources to buy our lamb. It had to be one without blemish. Because it was his first Passover at the Temple, we selected Yeshua to choose our lamb. Yosef carried it on his shoulders and went with my father. The women and girls, and boys who were under thirteen went into the Court of Women. Everybody else followed my father and Yosef into the Court of Israel and then to the altar.

I carefully watched the sacrificing of the lamb, as that is what I would be doing in a few years. My father performed the ritual quickly; it died instantly. He evoked prayers for the household that would celebrate the Passover Seder with this lamb. My father handed it back to Yosef. He, Zebedee and the other members of our group deemed to be adults left the altar area and rejoined us. My father stayed to perform the sacrifice ritual for other families. He planned to go back to the Zebedee house before sundown for the start of Passover.

As we went through the Court of the Gentiles, I asked Yosef if Yeshua and I could stay at the Temple and spend some time with the Masters. Yosef thought for a moment, and then agreed that we could stay as long as we returned to the house with my father.

I grabbed Yeshua by the hand and said, "This way." We ran to the part of the Temple and courtyard where my teachers would be holding instructions. I stopped instantly as we entered the area; a session was already underway. We grabbed a spot on the top stair and sat down.

We were in luck. Both my teachers, Master Yosef of Arimathea and a new teacher, Master Nicodemus, were there. They took turns telling parts of the story about our release from slavery in Egypt. The two Pharisees took us on a journey of mind and soul as they conveyed the Exodus story in all its richness.

I looked over at Yeshua, who sat wide-eyed with his face between his hands, totally focused on the storytellers. He must have sensed my stare because he turned and looked at me: "Aren't they wonderful? I hope someday that I will be able to tell stories as well as they do."

There were many more stories and lessons given until late afternoon. If it had been up to us, we would have stayed there until the evening. Master Yosef and Master Nicodemus knew better. We all had to join our families before sundown for the Passover Seder. The masters dismissed us after a quick series of testing questions.

As I headed out to find my father, Yeshua indicated he wanted to speak with the teachers. I met up with Father, and we waited for Yeshua to join us for the walk back to the house. The time was getting on, and my father was growing impatient. We eventually went looking for him. We found him holding court with Yosef and Nicodemus. My father thanked them for their "attentiveness to these young inquisitive minds," and wished them "Shalom."

"Shalom, I'll come again," Yeshua shouted over his shoulder as we left. Father looked back and bowed his head again, and hastened our pace to the Zebedee house.

***

The smell of roasting lamb, freshly cooked unleavened bread, and rich bitter and sweet spices teased our senses as we walked up the street. My mouth watered, and my stomach made such loud noises that Yeshua looked at me, "You're hungry. I'm right there with you," he said as he rubbed his stomach. "But remember the Passover meal is not about feeding the hunger of our bodies for food, but the hunger of our souls for God."

"Yes I know, and to remember what Adonai did for our people." I responded trying to sound wise even though I was surprised at the depth and truth behind his words.

Upon entering the house, we each performed the oblations required of us before we ascended the stairs to the Upper Room. Zebedee sat at the head with everyone else in their place on their cushion. The youngest person at the Seder begins the ritual meal with the question, *"Why is tonight different from all other nights?"* At our meal, that person was Suzanna, daughter of Zebedee and Salome. We celebrated the ritual meal with due reverence and in keeping with the traditions of our people.

After the Seder was finished, we would generally make way for people to sleep. Yeshua, however, had other plans as he tapped me on the shoulder and pointed at the roof. He wanted to pray, and as I was soon to discover, he wanted to pass the night in prayer. I could scarcely believe it. I was so full of Passover wine, our very finest I might add, that I could barely keep my eyes open.

"There will be lots of time for sleep," he said. "This is the perfect opportunity to pray for our people, that they will be open to receiving the Anointed One when he comes."

"All right, but I'm…" I did not dare finish what I wanted to say. "*I'm too tired*!"

I climbed the stairs with him again, but not with any enthusiasm. I literally dragged myself up there. We knelt in our favorite spots at the center of the roof. Yeshua prayed the psalms with great devotion. I tried to keep up with my part, but my brain would not focus, not tonight.

***

The cold morning air surrounded my body. I shivered, and in disturbed sleep, I attempted to pull the covers over me, only to find there were no covers. I was so tired I did not even want to open my eyes to find out why they were not within reach. Reluctantly, I opened one eye to discover I was on the roof. I had not gone to bed. I lifted my head to see Yeshua still sitting back on his heels in prayer. I let out some kind of groan. He turned his bowed head in my direction and smiled.

"Good morning, my friend. I trust you had a good sleep."

"Did you stay up all night praying?" I asked him even though I knew the answer.

"Yes."

"You must be exhausted."

"I have rested with my Father. He gives rest to my weary body and refreshes my soul."

Still, in a wine-fogged state of mind, I thought I heard Yeshua refer to God as "my Father." Maybe this is what his brothers referred to as "Yeshua, going all weird." He had a different way of speaking about the things of God.

I stretched out on the roof trying to pull the knots out of my back. Yeshua chuckled at me as I laid there in obvious discomfort. He stood, and held out his hand. I grabbed it; he pulled me to my feet as my back made cracking noises in protest.

"Ah," I said, as I shook my head against the cool wind that blew across the roof. "That feels good."

"Are you ready for breakfast?" he asked.

"Yes, I'm starved."

We headed back down the stairs where people still slept, except for Myriam and Salome, who were preparing breakfast. Yeshua went over to his mother, stood on his tiptoes and kissed her cheek; he did the same to his aunt. They were a close-knit family, that much was apparent. At twelve years old, Yeshua was a thoughtful person, something for me to emulate. I could not remember the last time I kissed my mother.

***

The day after the formal Passover celebration, Zebedee took us on a tour around Jerusalem. It was crowded with people, animals and wares from all over. We stayed in a tight group as we strolled through the big Jerusalem market. The mixture of food and animal smells was almost sickening.

Zebedee, because of his business arrangements, had access to the Roman governor's palace, and today he had a delivery to make. James hauled the cart loaded with several bags of smoked and salted fish for the Roman court. I thought it rather strange that Jews would do business so openly with the Romans until my father wondered if he could sell the remainder of our wine to the Romans. Zebedee shrugged and said, "It's worth a try."

We waited outside the Palace gate until the guard came and spoke to Zebedee, who indicated that we were with him. The guard took us to the Chief Steward's office. The steward, seated behind a desk, stood up to greet Zebedee as we entered the room.

"Shalom Zebedee, I trust you had a good Passover." The steward said as he shook Zebedee's hand.

"Shalom Marcus. We had an excellent celebration with a full house," Zebedee responded. He then introduced all of us to Steward Marcus. Zebedee and Marcus engaged in some business chatter and signed off on the exchange of the fish for appropriate monetary compensation.

While my father made his sales pitch to Chief Steward Marcus, I glanced around the office, which was a sparsely furnished room with a large banner of Caesar draped across the wall behind the desk. I looked out the door and saw Yeshua strolling around the area called the Pavement. He appeared headed for the Praetorium, a part of the palace that we are forbidden to enter during Passover. I made chase.

"We aren't supposed to go in there," I said as I caught up with him.

"How come?" Yeshua asked.

"We'd be defiled."

"Why is that?"

"It's one of the rules that a person defiles themselves if they step into the Judgement Hall of the pagans. I think it's because that's where they pronounce people guilty and send them to be crucified," I replied adding, "You don't ever want to go in there."

Yeshua shrugged and proceeded to the Hall. I did not follow him. I glanced over my shoulder to see if anyone was watching us. Yosef was indeed watching. He stepped outside.

"Yeshua, come out of there. That is not a place we should go," Yosef said to him.

"I was wondering if Governor Gratus was around."

"I'm sure he would receive you, Yeshua," I sneered. He just shook his head at me.

"We are finished here. Come boys," my father said.

"Did you sell any of the wine to the steward, Abba?" I asked.

"He took a taste, bought all the flasks, and paid well too," my father responded, "He asked that I be their wine supplier. He said that it was the best wine he has ever had from around here.

Chapter 4 My Father's Business

The days of Passover celebrations ended, and we all prepared to head back to our homes. There were no classes in the Temple the week after Passover, so I spent it at home. I was glad. I had much work to do in the vineyard, and this was an excellent opportunity to catch up on it before the growing season began in earnest.

The end of Passover meant saying goodbye to my new friend, Yeshua. He promised that we would see each other again, perhaps before next year's Passover. I hoped so, but Nazareth was a long way from Bethany. We would have to make a concerted effort to see each other before next year. We embraced and bid each other farewell. I admit I had a lump in my throat. I would miss him.

***

It was mid-afternoon a day or so after we had returned home when I heard my father's urgent call.

"Lazarus, can you come to the house right away?" I thought something must have happened to my mother. I dropped my pruning shears and ran into the house from the vineyard.

My heart was in my throat as I stepped through the door. Then I saw Yosef and Myriam, standing in our living area. Myriam was grey and shaking. Yosef looked frantic.

"Have you seen Yeshua?" Father asked.

"Not since we left Jerusalem, Abba," I replied, "Why, what's happened?"

Yosef spoke, "We were a day's journey from Jerusalem when we discovered Yeshua was not in the caravan with any of our family. He was not with us, and we assumed he was with Zebedee's family further along in the caravan. It was not until this morning that we discovered he was not with them. So we turned back and came here hoping he was with you."

His words were almost pleading as his voice trailed off. He was breathing heavily in apparent distress.

Myriam asked me, "Do you have any idea where he would be? Did he tell you where he was going?"

I shook my head, "No, I assumed he was going home with you. That's the impression I got when we parted."

"We must go back and find him. God knows he shouldn't be alone in Jerusalem; it is far too dangerous for a young lad," my father said. "Myriam you can stay here and wait for us to bring him back."

"No, I must go with you. I must find my son," she said choking back her tears.

I started out the door with my father, Yosef, and Myriam; however, I stopped and turned around and gave my mother a kiss on the cheek telling her I would be back. She was surprised and with a smile patted my face.

Bethany is relatively close to Jerusalem, but at that moment, it did not seem close enough. The four of us practically ran along the road. Yosef was breathing hard. My father suggested we slow our

E. Ann McIntyre

pace. We did. As we went, we discussed where we should begin our search.

We went directly to the Zebedee house. We checked the first level and the Upper Room. I was hoping he was on the roof, our favorite place of the house, but no. I stared briefly at the Temple; I remembered how Yeshua had told Masters Yosef and Nicodemus '*I'll come again*.' and then it hit me: *My teachers; I bet he is with my teachers.*

I tore down the stairs and announced my revelation to Yosef and Myriam. "I do hope you are right my son," my father said as we made our way back to the Temple.

We rushed into the Court of the Gentiles, and I made a beeline for the courtyard of the school. I got there before anyone else. I froze. He was there. Yeshua was once again holding court with Masters Yosef of Arimathea and Nicodemus. I felt sick.

My father, Yosef, and Myriam came in behind me. I looked into their faces. What I saw were part relief and part anger. Father and I retreated to the courtyard entrance as Myriam went to her son.

Yeshua had a surprised look on his face when he saw his mother. Myriam spoke, "My son we have been looking all over for you. Why have you done this to us? Your father and I have been worried sick."

"Why have you been so concerned?" Yeshua replied, "Did you not know I must be about my Father's business?"

I thought *What kind of response is that? Your father is a carpenter.* I glanced over at Yosef; he looked crestfallen. He had been so upset, so concerned about Yeshua's disappearance and now this. My father put his hand on my shoulder and led me out of the courtyard, "This is not our business."

While we waited in the outer court, Father suggested we invite them to stay in our guesthouse overnight because it was too late for them to start their journey back to Nazareth.

"We mustn't speak of this to them. They'll need to work this out," my father said.

***

During the trip back to Bethany, the tension was palpable. Father and I walked ahead with Yosef, Myriam, and Yeshua behind us. Once I turned around to see Yeshua looking back at the city. I thought, *Doesn't he understand what happened here? He still seems oblivious to the trouble he caused.*

When we arrived home, Father asked Martha to prepare our guesthouse for our visitors. She was happy to do so and invited our sister Miriam to help her. Miriam stood quietly in the corner eyeing Yeshua, paying little attention to Martha's invitation. Martha shrugged and went off by herself to prepare the small house.

"It is very kind of you to invite us to stay here tonight. I hope we are not burdening you with our presence," Yosef said.

"Oh heavens no," my father replied.

"Ester, I will help you with supper," Myriam of Nazareth offered to my mother.

"Thank you, Myriam. We have plenty and with the two of us, it won't take long to prepare."

Yeshua and I were standing there feeling somewhat uncomfortable. To break the tension, I invited him to join me up in the vineyard. Yeshua turned to Yosef and asked his permission.

"Yosef, may I go into the vineyard with Lazarus?"

That's strange, why does he call his father by his name? I thought.

"Yes, you may but come back in plenty of time for supper," Yosef replied. Yeshua went to Yosef, who sat with my father, put his arms around him and kissed his beard. Yosef hugged Yeshua, patted his face, and said, "Shalom, my son." His eyes glistened. Yosef smiled, took a deep breath, and looked off into the distance as if he remembered something. The tension in the room dissolved.

***

We ran up the path to the vineyard, which was about thirty feet from the house. It stretched up the hill and ran the full width of our property. I took Yeshua up to the crown of the hill, which had a large clearing between the vines, so we could take in the view from the hilltop.

"Wow," he said, "You can see Jerusalem. It's beautiful from here."

"Yes, I come up here to pray sometimes," I said. I really wanted to ask him why he did not call Yosef "Abba" or "Father," but I felt that I should heed my father's suggestion that we stay out of their family business.

We stood quietly taking in the vista of the sun setting behind the city.

"Yosef is not my father," Yeshua said softly as if he knew the questions I had in my head. "He married my mother shortly before I was born. He has raised me as his own and I love him dearly. I just wanted you to know."

In our custom, an unmarried man could marry his brother's widow or other family member's widow. I assumed that this was the circumstance in Yeshua's case.

"I wasn't going to pry, but I was wondering," I replied, "Is he your uncle?"

"No, he took my mother as his wife under unusual circumstances," Yeshua said, still looking at the distant outline of Jerusalem.

"So tell me, how do you grow the grapes that produce the best Passover wine around?" Yeshua asked, abruptly changing the subject.

I showed him the pruning process, how we graft vine branches together to produce different and better grapes. He was fascinated.

"So a good vine produces good fruit and a bad vine produces bad or no fruit," he said, summarizing my how-to-produce-good-grapes instructions.

"You got it!" I said with a laugh.

"I will remember what you have told me, Lazarus. It will be useful information to know someday, I'm sure."

"Yes, if carpentry doesn't work out you can always try growing a vineyard. Just not around these parts, I couldn't take the competition," I said laughing. He laughed too.

My inner senses told me it was time to head back to the house for supper. We arrived home just as mother called everyone to take their places. Yeshua and I sat next to each other.

In our family, we hold hands during the blessing before meals. Before he invoked the blessing, my father invited our guests to hold hands during the prayer. Yeshua took my hand in his. I took my sister

Miriam's hand. She smiled and looked passed me at Yeshua. *Oh my*, I thought, *Yeshua has a young admirer*. He winked at her. Miriam blushed and grinned.

Our mealtime passed with joyful conversation. Everyone laughed as Yeshua told them that I had revealed our family's grape-growing secrets. Father indicated he was not too worried about the impending competition from Galilee.

After supper, we bid each other "Shalom and a good night." My father walked Yosef and his family out to the guesthouse. I headed to my room, which was on the roof and threw myself on my cot. I was exhausted.

As tired as I was, my head was swimming with the day's events, and questions I still had about Yeshua. What he said to his mother of "*being about my father's business*" troubled me. *He must know who his father was and what he did for a living. Maybe he was a rabbi*. I thought to myself. Before I could think another thought, sleep overcame me.

***

The next morning I managed to sleep in a few extra minute. I had not intended to, but my early mornings with Yeshua during Passover had caught up with me. My father had to speak to me before I stirred.

"Lazarus, our guests are getting ready to leave. I'm sure you want to say farewell to your friend."

I bolted from my bed as if it was on fire. I practically fell down the stairs to the living area still wearing my sleeping gown. My father threw his cloak on me. Everyone laughed.

"I told them not to wake you for breakfast. I knew that my early mornings were not your style, and that I had exhausted you," Yeshua said.

"When will we see each other again?" I asked almost choking on my words. "It's not like we live next door to each other."

"Well, perhaps you can come up to Nazareth for my thirteenth birthday celebration in six months' time?" Yeshua suggested.

"Abba?" I said looking at my Father.

"We'll see. As long as you have completed this year's studies, it might be a good experience for you before your own celebration," he said.

"You are more than welcome to come," Yosef said with a smile adding, "We could use some of your lovely wine for the celebration."

I wrapped father's cloak tightly around me as we walked our guests to the town center to meet up with a northbound caravan. There were hugs all around as they boarded the cart.

We watched and waved as they headed out of sight. "They are a lovely family," Mother said, "I hope we do get to see them again."

"I do too," Miriam said.

"Somebody has a crush on Yeshua," I said with a laugh.

"I do not," Miriam replied, as she ran ahead of us toward the house.

"Now now, Lazarus, don't tease your sister," Mother said.

Martha darted ahead to catch up with Miriam. "Now there is someone I wish would get interested in Yeshua - or any other boy for that matter," Father said.

"What do you mean?"

"I asked Yosef. Yeshua does not have a contract. However, I guess he is not Martha's type. Whatever that is."

"Abba!" I shot back. "Not my friend. Besides he is too young for Martha."

"He's too *from Nazareth*" for Martha, or so she told me," Father said.

I just shook my head. At fifteen years old with no betrothal contract, I knew my parents were getting concerned. They were not the type of people to force a daughter or son to marry someone they did not want to marry. Nevertheless, that stance had its limits. Martha would have to settle for someone soon. I just did not want that someone to be my best friend - ever.

Chapter 5 Valley of Tears

It started out a normal summer day. Father went to the Temple for a meeting with the priests. Mother and Martha were making bread, the aroma wafting its way up to the vineyard, where I was busy pruning with my constant companion, Miriam, at my side.

Martha's scream reverberated all the way up the hill, "Lazarus, Lazarus!" I scooped Miriam up in my arms, raced down the path through the courtyard, and into the house. I saw Martha bent over my mother on the floor. Martha was sobbing so hard she could not speak. It was apparent to me, even without touching her, that Mother was dead. Miriam immediately joined Martha on the floor pawing my mother's body, shaking her, telling her to wake up.

In spite of my own grief, I wrapped my arms around my sisters to comfort them - an impossible task. I covered my mother's body with a blanket from my parents' bedroom and settled my sisters on the cushions near her body. Martha held Miriam in her arms, rocking back and forth, and hummed a sorrowful tune.

***

It had to be the worst trip to Jerusalem I ever made. I rushed to the building where the priests held their meeting. The door was open. I stood in the entrance; my father sat directly across from me.

Before I even got a word out, he rushed by and grabbed me by my hand as he went. He knew. We never spoke a word as we hurried back to Bethany. He held my hand so tightly I thought my fingers would fall off.

***

The days of mourning and burial of my mother are a blur. We had many mourners come from Jerusalem and the surrounding area. Out of respect for my father, the whole Sanhedrin came. My parents were well-known respected members of the community. We buried Mother outside of Bethany in the designated burial grounds on the side of a hill. The sepulchre was a family crypt built by my grandfather for his family and future generations.

Until the death of my mother, I had never known the sadness, the terrible grief of losing someone so close to me. In public, I went through the motions of what was required of me. It was in the aloneness of my room that it hit me. I was angry with God for taking my mother. She was too young to die. She would miss my Son of the Commandment ceremony, my becoming a priest in a few years. I was so angry that I decided that I would punish God by not saying my prayers or talking to him in any way.

The effect on my sisters was equally traumatic. Martha found herself suddenly thrust into the "mother" role. A role she loved to play, except now, it was not play. My father immediately began relying on her to manage the household, take care of Miriam, and make a comfortable home for us.

The impact on Miriam was not immediately apparent. It was clear she was grieving our mother.

She was always quiet in nature, but I was too caught up in my own grief to notice that my little sister was turning inward on herself. She needed her brother and sister, but neither one of us were there for her.

Father seemed distracted, almost aimless after my mother's death. He wouldn't go to the Temple for days on end. He told me he felt duty-bound to be home for his children and yet obliged to be at the temple. I was twelve, almost thirteen; I had no right answers for him. I went to Temple because I had to study and prepare for my life as a man under God's Law. I was in some ways lucky to have that as a focus in my life. Time was marching on. I would turn thirteen in five months, ready or not.

**

A month after my mother's death there was a delivery.

We all gathered around as Father unwrapped the brown leather pouch, exposing a single-page letter. I looked over Abba's right arm and read along with him.

"Boethius bar Simeon,

I hope this letter finds you and your family well. My wife Myriam and I invite you and your family to Nazareth for Yeshua's thirteenth birthday celebration. It will take place on Parashat, Vayeilech. We have plenty of room within our family homes so please do not worry about a place to stay.

We look forward to your coming to this special occasion.

Your friends Yosef, Myriam, and Yeshua"

31

E. Ann McIntyre

I stared wide-eyed at my father. Yosef, of course, had no way of knowing about my mother's death. I knew that such a trip was out of the question now, even though I so wanted to go.

Abba dropped his hand holding the letter. He shook his head, rubbed his beard, and took a deep breath. My Abba's eyes filled with the first tears I had seen in his eyes since Mother died. I teared-up too and my throat tightened.

"Your mother was very excited about going to Nazareth for this celebration. She truly wanted to get together with Myriam again. I think that she would want us to go, I honestly do."

"Are you certain, Abba?" I said in a low voice trying not to sound too excited.

"I am. And not just because Yeshua is your friend, but because I think this trip would do all of us a great deal of good."

I wiped my eyes.

"Martha, you can organize what needs to be done for this journey. You just tell us what you need us to do and everyone will help you. That's what your mother would do," he said.

Martha's eyes widened as a smile grew on her face. Even Miriam was biting her lower lip and bouncing on her toes with excitement. Abba gave each one of us a hug. The letter from Nazareth had breathed life back into our family.

I turned on my heels and ran up to the vineyard to the clearing where Yeshua and I had stood a few months earlier. I faced Jerusalem and broke my silence with God. I prayed, "Thank you!"

Chapter 6 The Journey North

Father arranged for a regular weekly northbound caravan to pick us up in Bethany's town center. I lost count of the number of times I packed and unpacked my haversack. Martha kept changing her mind about what we each needed to take with us to Nazareth. Abba was losing patience.

"We have one hour to get to the town center, come on Martha, make a decision and stick to it," he said in his ever-tender but insistent voice.

"There, all right, we're done. I think we have everything we need," Martha replied, "Wait, Miriam do you have..."

"Martha we are going now!" Father said. He trooped us out the door, pushing Martha by the shoulders ahead of him. I smirked.

***

The caravan consisted of six carts: two carried passengers, and four carried goods. There were three donkeys carrying food, water, and tents, plus the ones pulling the carts. There were four men on horseback; one was the owner, and the other three men were protectors. The destination of this caravan was the City of Sepphoris, three miles from Nazareth.

Our family boarded one cart. Pulled by a mule, the cart had a partial wooden covering for protection from the elements. The ride was not comfortable.

Thanks to the Romans use of paving stones, I had to sit on my haversack to keep from getting a sore bum, a minor inconvenience considering the adventurous journey ahead.

As we headed north and left the City of Jerusalem behind, I turned around to take in the beautiful view of the city. I held Miriam in place as she stood on the cart to get a better look. Father smiled at the sight of his children enjoying the journey and in some ways a new life. We did not forget our mother, not at all; it was as if she was with us. Moreover, as Father had said, she wanted us to go. We were a family at peace.

Father had made enough money from sales of our wine to the Governor's Palace that we would not have to sleep in the caravan tents. We would avail ourselves of the inns along the roadside when we stopped for the night. We would be two nights and three days on the road to Nazareth.

Our first stop was Arimathea, the hometown of Master Yosef. We stopped outside the inn at the edge of town. It had room for the caravan to set up for the night. The inn was a decent size and well prepared by its keepers to receive travellers like us. Father negotiated a good size room that would accommodate the four of us. Martha brought along sufficient food for us to enjoy a full supper before bedding down for our first night on the road.

I laid awake for a little while thinking over the day. I wanted to remember every detail of my first journey away from home. It was funny really; the one thing I noted was *what straight roads the Romans made.* I chuckled to myself and rolled over fast asleep.

We woke early the next morning to a breakfast provided by the innkeepers. It was quite a feast of breads, cheese, and fruit. They even provided us with a lunch for later.

"What a blessing this is for us," Martha said, "we won't have to use our food." Martha was invariably concerned about food, either not having enough or having too much. However, it always worked out just right.

The caravan followed the wide Roman road northwest toward the Great Sea. Our next stop was Caesarea, the Roman capital of Judea, situated by the sea with a port to accommodate ships from Rome. I had never seen the sea before. I was excited.

"Abba will we be able to walk by the sea and put our feet in the water?" I asked.

"I don't know son; I will ask the drivers."

The reply came back that the place where we would be stopping was an inn right along the shore, just outside of Caesarea. I could not believe our luck.

There were many other caravans on the road going both east and west. We were travelling a major trade route. There were also a number of Roman soldiers, "just out keeping the peace," or so they said. They only stopped us once to look at the caravan owner's merchant papers.

Early in the afternoon, the caravan stopped to water the animals and allow everyone to have lunch. I took in the changing scenery around us. The land was getting flatter, so I could see for miles. Ahead of us, I could just barely make out the deep-blue strip of sea along the horizon. To the north, I could see a gentle wave of hills, not unlike the hills of Judea. It was

E. Ann McIntyre

beautiful. After lunch, we headed out again toward the blue strip on the horizon.

**

I stood on the wet sand with my sandals in my hands. I looked out at the sea as the waves tickled my feet. Miriam started running; Martha did too, and I dropped my sandals and ran with them. Running on the beach was an amazing experience until I fell flat on my face. My sisters took my hands and tried to get me on my feet. I was laughing too hard to get up. We eventually went back to Father, who quietly strolled the beach laughing at us. He gave us all a hug and led us to the inn for our supper.

After supper, Abba asked me if I wanted to go down to the beach again and recite our evening prayers. I was delighted to have a chance to pray with my father on the beach. Father had his prayer shawl, so he led the prayer. I did not have mine yet. I would receive mine on my thirteenth birthday. The thought crossed my mind as we started our prayer that Mother would have made my prayer shawl on her loom, but that would not happen now. I figured Father would have to purchase one for me.

**

The next morning we waited around while the caravan owner picked up some more goods at the Roman pier. There were a number of packages destined for Sepphoris, the provincial capital of Galilee. Once the cargo was loaded and secured on one of the carts, we all boarded, and the caravan headed northeast.

The further inland we went the more mountainous the terrain became. Off to the left in the distance, I could see a high mountain range. Abba saw me looking at it.

"That is Carmel, the sacred mountain of the prophet Elijah," he said. "That is where the sword of Elijah brought fire down from Heaven against the pagan god Baal and scorched the earth. We can't go there now, but maybe someday we can make a pilgrimage to the very spot."

"Abba, I would love that," I replied.

"The valley we are about to go through is called the Jezreel Valley. This whole area is very rich and fertile. Grapes and other such crops grow in abundance here," he said.

"I don't think I've seen so much greenery growing over such a wide area," I said. In Judea, we had to water daily to get our vines to grow and be fruitful. We were always fighting to stave off the desert. Here the growth was naturally abundant.

This part of the journey was the longest stretch. We did stop briefly to water the animals but we had to eat on the go. Martha was well prepared as we dug into the food she had brought for our journey. The drivers assured us that we were making good time. We would be at our Nazareth stop before supper. I hoped so because frankly, we seem to be going a bit faster and the ride was getting even more uncomfortable.

As the day grew shorter, the driver pointed to the hillside ahead of us, "There she is, Nazareth!"

I strained to see through the haze. Sure enough, glimmering in the late afternoon sun, I could see a

E. Ann McIntyre

small village. "*Finally*," I said to myself. "*I hope we can find Yosef's house.*" I need not have worried.

As we came to a small road just below the village, I saw someone standing and waving at us. It was Yeshua; I waved heartily back and called to him. "Yeshua, Yeshua, we are here, we made it!"

Yeshua ran down to meet us. The caravan had barely come to a halt when I jumped off the cart, nearly knocking Yeshua down.

"Shalom, Shalom!" we greeted each other, slapping each other's backs.

Yeshua welcomed my father and sisters, then very insistently, took their bags. I carried my own. As we headed up to the village, Yeshua extended his condolences to us on our mother's death; Father had mentioned it in the letter of response to their invitation. Yeshua also told us we would be staying with his grandmother Anna. His grandfather Joachim had died a few years ago.

We went through the small village center where there was a well and a few food stalls. It was not unlike Bethany. Yeshua pointed to a small house where an elderly woman stood waiting. As we approached, Yosef and Myriam came out of the house and waved to us.

There were cheerful greetings all around. Martha and Miriam were shown to their room, which was the same room that Myriam and her sister Salome shared when they were growing up. Yosef took Father and me to the roof where Joachim had built an enclosure for overnight guests. It was small but out of the elements and quite comfortable. Yosef invited us to come down for supper as soon as we settled in.

I stood on the roof to look at the spectacular view of the valley in the setting sun. I could hear sheep nearby. I walked to the back edge of the roof and saw Yeshua herding a number of sheep into a holding pen behind the house. He closed the gate and walked out into the field beyond my view. I watched for a little while longer and saw him come back carrying a young lamb across his shoulders. He opened the gate of the sheepfold and carefully put the young animal down. He must have sensed he was being watched; he looked up at me and waved. I waved back and turned to go downstairs for supper. *Yeshua is a shepherd too,* I thought.

Yosef and Miriam excused themselves from having supper with us as they had a crowd for supper at their own home a short distance away.

"However," Yosef said as he put his hand on Yeshua shoulder, "this young man, I mean almost young man, has been begging all day to have supper here with you. So he will. We will see you all tomorrow at the synagogue. Yeshua, do not be late coming home, you have a big day tomorrow."

"I won't and thank you for making this time so special for me, Yosef."

I sat down on a cushion fully expecting Yeshua to sit next to me, but to my astonishment, he invited Martha to sit, and he helped his grandmother serve the meal. I think he saw my mouth fall open in shock.

"You are our guests; I am here to serve you." He grinned as Grandmother Anna tousled his hair. "Nice to see my daughter is raising you so well," she said.

After he served everyone, Yeshua did indeed sit next to me. Anna invited my father to invoke the blessing. We had a grand meal with Anna as a

E. Ann McIntyre

wonderful host. She told us that she was very grateful that Yeshua could spend so much time with her. Since her husband died, it was hard for her to care for the sheep. She thought she would have to sell them until Yeshua took over their care. "I use their wool to make yarn which I sell in the market. It keeps me comfortable." Widows who are alone do not fare well unless they have someone to care for them and protect them from thieves. Yeshua was his grandmother's protector just by looking after her sheep.

After the meal, Yeshua helped his grandmother clean up and then escorted her to her room. Her walking ability was limited somewhat, so his strong arm steadied her. Martha watched carefully and said that she would assist Anna as needed tomorrow during the celebration.

Yeshua and I had a lot of catching up to do, not the least of which was that he was about to become a "Son of the Commandment" in the eyes of all of Israel. I would too, in a couple of months, but right now, it was his turn. I was very anxious to talk to him, however, night had fallen and it was time for him to be getting home. Our chat would have to wait until after the ceremony.

Chapter 7 Yeshua: Son of Israel

Morning was preparation time. Anna took a carefully wrapped item out from a shelf behind her loom. She untied the string that held the white cloth in place and exposed a beautiful white and blue striped prayer shawl. She opened the shawl up and began inspecting it for flaws as if it was possible there would be any. Anna ran her finger over the entire front and back surface of the garment until she was satisfied that it was perfect. Next, she checked the fringes on both corners making sure they were the same size. Folding the shawl in two, end-to-end, Anna held it up for us to see.

"It's beautiful Anna. Yeshua will love it!" I said.

Anna smiled and nodded, "Thank you, I wanted to make a special shawl for my grandson."

Anna folded the shawl, wrapped it up in the white cloth, and indicated she would give it to Yosef to put over Yeshua's shoulders during the ceremony. Just as she tucked it back on the shelf, the door opened.

"Good morning everyone," Yeshua said.

We must have looked guilty because Yeshua got an inquisitive look on his face and said, "Did I interrupt something?"

We all went into denial and lined up to block Yeshua's view of the shelf. We burst out laughing as Anna stepped around us and gave Yeshua a big hug.

"Yom huledet sameach," [Happy Birthday], Yeshua my dear grandson," she said.

"Todah Savta, [Thank you Grandmother]," Yeshua responded in his grandmother's embrace.

"Yom huledet sameach Yeshua," We all said in unison as we gathered around him. I gave him a hug too.

"Thank you, everyone," he said.

"Lazarus, I thought you might like to help me with the sheep this morning."

"I'd love to. I don't know anything about sheep," I said, "Except that they feed and clothe us."

Yeshua led the way out back to the sheep hold. "We'll feed them some grain before we put them out to pasture," he said as he filled a couple of buckets with grain from a bin just outside the pen. He gave me one and opened the gate, taking care not to let any of the sheep get by him as he ushered me in past him.

The sheep butted against my knees trying to get at the grain. One aggressive creature stuck her whole head in the bucket and forced it from my hand, spilling the contents on the ground. Yeshua held on to his bucket and laughed, "That's all right; they'll eat it off the ground."

After the sheep got their feed of grain, Yeshua took a collar with a bell on it and selected an older ewe to put it on. "She will be the leader of the herd today; the rest will follow her around," Yeshua said. He took the lead sheep out of the pen and sure enough, the others followed her as she followed Yeshua. It was amazing to watch them all line up behind Yeshua as he walked out into the pasture. *The shepherd leading his flock* I thought to myself. I fell in behind the last sheep, which happened to be a lamb. Yeshua stopped in the middle of the field and let the ewe graze. The herd of about 30 sheep spread out around us.

"There's one more thing we need to do. We need to bring out the herd's protector."

"Their protector?"

"Yes, and Jenny does a fine job protecting the sheep. Come, Lazarus, we'll go and get her."

I was not sure what to expect. I thought that maybe Yeshua had hired someone to look after the sheep. We walked around the house to the other side where there was another pen. This pen held a couple of donkeys, a jenny and her foal. Yeshua looked at me with a bemused smile on his face.

"This is the protector of all woolly creatures? You're joking. Right?"

"No," he said, "A donkey will take out any coyote or even a lone wolf that might threaten the sheep. They are a shepherd's best friend." He took the donkey by its halter and led it out, with the foal following behind, to the field where the sheep grazed. I chalked it up as a learning experience and not just about sheep.

***

The small synagogue filled to capacity well before the special service for Yeshua began. This was an occasion when I was particularly annoyed at not being able to stand with the men during a celebration. I was twelve and still had to sit with the women. Yeshua's mother Myriam was very kind and had me stand with her during the service with Anna standing next to me. I felt as though I was Yeshua's brother.

E. Ann McIntyre

I peered through the grate that separated the men and the women during services. I watched with a lump in my throat as Yeshua received Anna's prayer shawl from Yosef; glancing up at Anna I could see she had tears in her eyes. Myriam rubbed my shoulder as Yeshua prepared to give his first reading from the scriptures in front of his whole town.

"Yeshua bar Yosef, please come forward to proclaim the Lord's Word," The Rabbi said as he placed a scroll on the podium.

Yeshua lifted his shawl on to his head, leaned forward, kissed the scroll, and opened it. As he proclaimed the Word to all of us, his wide eyes scanned the entire room, including the grated area where he looked right at me. I felt goosebumps all over as his voice filled the room. Yeshua proclaimed the prophet's words as though they were his own. I was impressed, to say the least.

The ceremony ended with Yosef praying a blessing over Yeshua as everyone extended their hands in his direction. Yeshua sported a big smile as he made his way through the crowd of well-wishers. His mother and grandmother met him at the door. He kissed and embraced them both. Then he embraced me and whispered, "You're next."

Chapter 8 Boys

The reception party took place at Yosef and Myriam's home not far from Anna's house. There were so many people that the attendees spilt over into the street and into the back garden, which is where Yeshua and I wound up, sitting on Yosef's bench located outside his workshop.

"I am not going to remain a carpenter like Yosef or my brothers," Yeshua said as he ran his hand over the smooth wood of the bench.

"What are you going to do?" I asked him.

"Teach."

"Teach what?"

"Teach all these people about God."

"How are you going to do that? Are you going to be a Rabbi?" I queried.

"Yes, but not the kind of Rabbi who teaches only in the Synagogue or in the Temple. I will go to the people and teach them where they are, be that in their homes or in their fields, or in their fishing boats," Yeshua explained.

"What makes you think people will even listen to you? You are only thirteen," I countered.

"I'm not talking about teaching now, but the time will come when I will do as my Father commands me."

Once again, Yeshua referred to God as Father and spoke as though he had a direct connection with God. I was confused, if not a little concerned about

E. Ann McIntyre

Yeshua's way of thinking. I had no idea how to respond to his statement. I was starting to think that maybe his brothers were right when they referred to him as "*going all weird*". The more he spoke to me about God, the more I wondered about him. I was from the old school of Jewish traditions; Yeshua was from his own school.

James bar Zebedee joined us on the bench. He had already had his thirteenth birthday, so he stood with the men during Yeshua's ceremony. He came from the house carrying a plate full of food, which we were more than happy to devour. He didn't seem to mind as we helped ourselves.

The three of us leaned against the wall of Yosef's workshop and watched, with some amusement, the activity around us. Young children chased the village dog through the courtyard, while adults talked endlessly about the ongoing tensions between the Romans and the Zealots who camped out in the hills.

James whispered to Yeshua, "The pond is full of water."

Yeshua grinned, "I don't suppose anyone will notice we are gone."

"Let's go. Come with us Lazarus, we are going to have some fun," James said.

We slipped out the back past the chicken coop. We ran up the hill behind the village and then ran down the other side. I had no idea where we were going. I followed James and Yeshua, apparently to the "pond".

We ascended a gentle knoll, and that is when I saw our destination, a small, somewhat murky pool of water. Running ahead, James and Yeshua threw off their clothes and plunged into the water. I tried to come to a complete halt on the edge of the pond, but my sandals slipped on the wet grass, and down I went on my rear. The other two burst out laughing and urged me to join them.

"What if someone comes along and we are caught without a stitch on?" I reasoned. That did not seem to faze them one bit. They just exhorted me to join them. Not wanting to feel left out, I ripped off my clothes and fell on my belly in the water. When I stood, the water was up to my waist.

I had to admit, it was fun splashing around in the increasingly muddy pool of water in total abandonment. I didn't do this kind of thing back in Bethany. I approached life a bit more on the serious side. This was indeed fun - until James suddenly stopped laughing, and a fearful look came over his face.

I turned and saw ten Roman soldiers on horseback picking up our clothes with their swords. My heart was in my throat. I thought we were about to die. We were in a dangerous situation.

The soldiers edged their horses toward the water so they could drink, all the while sitting on their mounts with big grins on their faces. One of the soldiers came forward; he appeared to be the Centurion of the group. He walked his horse around us. He put the tip of his sword against my neck. Terrified, I closed my eyes and waited for the sword to slit my throat.

"I have a son about your age if he was here I bet he'd be doing the same thing," he said.

"Centurion Marius, shall we spare them today?" one of the soldiers asked.

E. Ann McIntyre

"Yes, it's a nice day for a swim in the mud. Besides, I think this young lad works with his father as a carpenter at my home, and I need them to finish the work," the Centurion said pointing to Yeshua. "Is that right young man?"

"Yes, sir, I do work there occasionally," Yeshua replied, "I know your son Gaius."

"Ah, I thought so. I've been telling him not to get too friendly with the Jewish boys because you never know when you might have to kill 'em," Centurion Marius said.

"My Father tells me that we should love our enemies, to do good to those who hurt us," Yeshua said.

"Well, that's an interesting approach. It might get you killed, but it is an interesting approach," the Centurion replied.

I kept looking between Yeshua and the soldier. I could not believe that Yeshua actually said what he just said. *Now I know he's crazy*, I thought.

"Come on men, let's move on." The Centurion motioned to his men and kicked his horse forward. They left, taking our clothes with them.

I almost passed out in relief.

Yeshua and James burst out laughing.

"I don't see what's so funny. I had a sword at my throat. I could have been killed," I said to them with great consternation, "and now we don't have any clothes!"

"Lazarus, Centurion Marius had no intention of killing you. He was teasing you!" Yeshua said, "I know him and his family, they are nice people."

"Well, I'm glad you think so. I do not see the humour in this at all."

"How are we going to get back with nothing on?" I asked anyone who might have an answer.

"We walk," Yeshua said as he got out of the water still wearing his loincloth.

"I am naked; I took everything off!" I replied. "This isn't going to go over well with my father I'm sure."

I was indignant, both Yeshua and James had their loincloths on.

James bent down and held up my loincloth. The soldiers hadn't taken it. "Want this?"

I was relieved, to say the least. "Yes, can you bring it to me?"

"You'll have to come and get it," James replied.

"Come on James, bring it to me please," I pleaded.

Yeshua walked passed James, grabbed my article of clothing and threw it to me. I caught it and made myself decent, not as proper as I wanted to be, but at least I was decent.

"How are we going to explain this to our parents?" I asked.

"We tell them the truth," Yeshua replied.

"This isn't going to go over well, I just know it," I said. "Although I can tell Father how brave I was when the soldier held the sword to my throat."

"Brave?" James said. "You were shaking like a leaf in the wind."

Yeshua walked up beside me and put his arm around my shoulders. "That's fine Lazarus; you had no way of knowing that he wasn't going to hurt you. You were right to be frightened, can't blame you for that. Tell your father the story the way you need to tell it... just don't lie."

***

I was right; "the muddy pond" incident did not
go over well. The three of us stood in front of our
respective parent, Yosef, Zebedee, and Boethius. It
was hard to tell who was angrier, but I would bet it
was Yosef. He did not find the whole Centurion
Marius encounter amusing at all.

"He is a Roman soldier; they crucify our people
without batting an eye. Don't ever think that because
we work for him that somehow makes us
untouchable. It doesn't."

"Yes, sir," Yeshua replied in a quiet voice.

After the formal scolding, they excused us and
told us to try to stay out of trouble the rest of the day.
Our fathers were going to say "the rest of the week",
but they thought that that requirement might be
impossible for us to keep. They were probably right.
I'm sure I caught a glimpse of my father with a grin
on his face. I think the three of them did find the
situation amusing. They turned their backs to us so
we could not see the smiles on their faces.

***

The next day Yeshua and I spent time at his
home and in Yosef's workshop. Yeshua had created
something for me. He explained that although he
worked on large building projects in Sepphoris with
Yosef and his brothers, he really liked working on
small woodworking projects. He lifted a tarp that
covered a piece on the workbench. I was amazed at
what I saw. It was a scale model of the Temple.

"Yeshua, it's wonderful. It looks perfect! How did you do it?" I asked him.

"Well, I just remembered what it looked like and I did an estimate of the dimensions and chiselled it out of a solid block of wood. Then I slowly carved out the detail of the temple," he explained. "I hope you like it!"

"I love it. I will treasure it forever!"

It took the two of us to carry the model into the house to show everyone. It was greeted with words of amazement and praise for Yeshua's skill. As we gathered around the Temple model, we heard the sound of horses coming into the village. It could only mean one thing... Romans.

Yosef closed the door as Myriam closeted the girls into a bedroom off the living area. Yosef held his finger to his lips to ensure our silence. Romans soldiers went through the streets of Bethany all the time, but we didn't hide in our homes, we just gave them a wide berth. I was beginning to understandd that here in the north there was a great deal of tension between our people and the Romans.

Yosef cracked the door open and peered down the street. The soldiers were coming our way. Yosef closed the door and waited. The horses stopped right in front of the house. Yosef stood by the door but did not open it. He gave us the shush sign again. I felt tense. I looked over at Yeshua. He stood with his eyes closed, his lips moved in silent prayer. I looked at my father who had his eyes fixed on Yosef. Zebedee was doing the same thing.

A knock on the door startled us. Yosef held his hand up to us.

"Who is it?' Yosef asked.

"Yosef, its Gaius Marius, I am here with my son Gaius." The Centurion we met at the pond the day before.

Yosef's demeanour visibly relaxed and he opened the door.

"Shalom Yosef, I have come with my son here to offer my apologies for the incident yesterday afternoon, when my soldiers and I encountered your son and a couple of his friends. It was not my intention to frighten them, and I think that perhaps I stepped over the line with one of the boys in particular. I would like to take this opportunity to make amends," Centurion Marius said.

Yosef open the door wider and invited them in. "Shalom, yes well, come in. The boys are here. Let me make some introductions."

The Centurion was not wearing his armour nor was he carrying any weapons that I could see. His son was about my height and carried what looked like clothes. Yosef introduced my father and Zebedee then James and me. I admit I was a little nervous, as I did not know what to expect.

Centurion Marius stepped forward and bowed slightly in my direction. "Lazarus, please accept my apologies for what I did yesterday. It might be acceptable to point a sword at an adult in combat but not at a child at play," he said.

I didn't know what to say. I fumbled with the words but I managed to spit out "Thank you."

"You're welcome, young man," he said. I was glad he changed his word "child" to "young man."

He turned to Yosef and said, "Yesterday your son Yeshua told me something you have taught him. I brushed it off at first but his words stayed with me and I really thought about it."

"Oh?" Yosef said as he glanced at Yeshua. "What did he tell you?"

"He said and I quote, "*My Father tells me that we should love our enemies, to do good to those who hurt us.*" Yosef looked in Yeshua's direction, rubbed his beard and said, "Aha". Yeshua bit his lower lip and looked sheepishly at Yosef.

Centurion Marius continued, "I think that is a courageous thing to teach your son. I have brought my son along to learn something from your family. We have some garments which I hope will replace the clothes that we took yesterday."

His son Gaius stepped forward and presented Yeshua, James, and I with the clothes he was carrying. We thanked him.

By that time Myriam, Martha, and Miriam had come out of the bedroom and were standing near Yeshua. Myriam reached out and took Yeshua under her arm.

"Centurion Marius, please join us for supper, we have so much left over from yesterday's celebration that we could feed an army," she said with a smile.

"Well thank you, but please call me Gaius," he said. "What celebration did you have yesterday?"

"It was Yeshua's thirteenth birthday," Yosef replied.

"That is an important one for you, isn't it? Happy Birthday, Yeshua," Gaius said.

"Yes thank you. You know about Jewish special occasions?" Yeshua asked.

"I do I do, I've been in this part of the Empire for almost twenty years. Young Gaius and his older brother were born in Sepphoris. So we've had time to familiarize ourselves with your customs."

E. Ann McIntyre

I couldn't believe that I was sharing supper with a Roman soldier and his son. Doing business with the Romans was one thing but this was very strange. Yeshua was delighted with the arrangement and carried on a lively conversation with young Gaius, who sat next to him. I listened to their conversation. I heard Yeshua giving his Roman friend another snippet of his wisdom.

"If you treat others as you want to be treated, you'll have more friends than enemies. If someone hits you on one cheek, turn the other cheek to him, and do not hit back," he said. Although he spoke quietly, all the adults dropped their conversations to listen to Yeshua.

"Your son seems to have more words of wisdom for us, Yosef. Is this more of your teaching?" Gaius asked.

"No, Yeshua comes up with these little sayings on his own," Yosef replied.

I looked at my father who had a frown on his face, and I knew why. What Yeshua had said on both occasions contradicted what our scriptures taught, "*An eye for an eye and a tooth for a tooth*". I suspected Father would have a talk with me about this on the way home.

***

We left Nazareth a couple of days after the landmark supper with the Roman family. Before we left Father had extended an invitation to Yosef, Myriam, and Yeshua to come to Bethany for my thirteenth birthday celebrations in a couple of months. They had already worked it into their plans and we were delighted that they would come.

Lazarus of Bethany

As I sat on the caravan cart, I carefully held on to the model of the Temple that Yeshua had created for me. I thought about him; what his friendship meant to me. Although I was concerned about Yeshua's so-called "*words of wisdom*", I felt strangely peaceful about the whole experience. Father had already warned me about paying too much attention to the talk of friends, rather than strict adherence to the teachings of scripture as given by my Masters at the Temple. I could see the inconsistency between those traditional teachings and the words of Yeshua. He also said things to me in private that my father never heard, and I kept them to myself. I knew it would strain our friendship if my father ever heard Yeshua referring to God as his "*Father*".

E. Ann McIntyre

Chapter 9 Becoming

"Its fuzz, just fuzz," I said to myself as I looked into the mirror at my chin for the hundredth time. It was only two days before my thirteenth birthday, and I was obsessed with my looks; my manly looks to be exact. Father told me that the beard, the voice change, and growth spurt would all come over the next few years. He said that being an adult under the Law was not the same as being physically a man. I must have had it explained to me several times by my Masters and by my father. Even so, I wanted to look mature at my coming of age ceremony. At least I had the hair on either side of my face trained to curl, not an easy task for someone with completely straight hair.

The guest list for my "Son of the Commandment" ceremony was quite lengthy, mainly because of my father's position as the High Priest. The entire Sanhedrin, plus other officials, my personal guests, and family members would be there. I was a nervous wreck. I paced the roof with a copy of the prophet's words, which I would read in front of everyone at the Temple. I remembered how confident Yeshua was when he read, if I could be half as good as him that would be an achievement. I had read these words so many times to myself or with my father or in class, I knew them off by heart, but having to get up in front of so many important people and read, or rather proclaim the sacred words, was daunting.

As I continued my feverish pacing and reading, I sensed someone was watching me. I spun around to see who it was. Yeshua.

"You are here early. I thought you were coming tomorrow!" I exclaimed with delight.

"We caught a caravan that was going south with no passengers, so they were happy to take us," Yeshua said as we greeted each other.

I sized him up and noted that he had already started his growth spurt. He didn't have his beard yet either, but he sure had gained a few inches on me in the last couple of months. He had let his hair grow too, so it was longer than mine was, but he did not have the curls by the sides of his face.

I told him how nervous I was about reading in front of everyone. He promised to pray for me so that I would be at peace. Somehow, just having Yeshua say that helped to calm my nerves.

We headed downstairs where I greeted Yosef and Myriam. Martha had prepared for our guests well in advance, so their early arrival didn't faze her a bit. She had already served them the fruits of our labor from the vineyard.

Yosef raised his goblet in toast, "To Lazarus, may the blessings of the Lord be with you."

"To Lazarus," they all said.

I blushed and smiled; I was so happy with their greeting.

We sat down to a wonderful supper Martha had prepared. Myriam helped serve while my sister Miriam took her usual stance of staring at Yeshua with a silly grin on her face.

Our families had a lot to catch up on, and we talked well into the evening. After supper, my father suggested that we go to the roof to recite our evening prayer. As we climbed the stairs, I noticed Yosef's laboured breathing; much as he had when we made the dash to Jerusalem to find Yeshua. Yeshua reached up behind Yosef to steady him. I could see the concern in his face.

Father led the prayer as we stood in a semi-circle facing Jerusalem. I felt very much at peace. My interior was calm for a change. It was a tremendous help when Father prayed for me, holding his hand over me as he did so.

***

The next morning as I dozed on my cot, I heard someone on the roof outside my bedroom. I knew immediately who it was, "Yeshua?" I said.

"Good morning. I was trying not to wake you," he said as he poked his head in the doorway.

"That's all right. I'm trying to get up early for morning prayers too. It's so peaceful this time of day," I said as I slowly got to my feet.

I joined Yeshua on the roof in the cool misty morning. Winter was coming so early-mornings were cooler and the rains came more frequently. We prayed as we had in Jerusalem during Passover. Our prayer together was natural; we were in spiritual communion with each other and God.

After our prayer time, I asked Yeshua about Yosef's health.

"Is Yosef unwell? He seemed short of breath last night, as he did when we went to Jerusalem to find you."

"He gets like that when we rush. It has been happening more frequently lately. I was a little concerned about him making this trip. However, he insisted that he would be all right," Yeshua told me.

"We take a cart to Sepphoris now when we go there to work. Yosef only works on parts of the job that don't require much exertion. Mostly he just directs us and manages the project."

"Do you think we should take our cart to Jerusalem when we go tomorrow? Would that be easier for him?

"Yes, that would probably be very helpful. I will tell my mother, she will be pleased. She has been very concerned too."

The smell of fresh warm bread and eggs invited us downstairs, where Martha and Myriam were making breakfast. Yeshua kissed his mother good morning. She smiled. I thought to myself *What a beautiful woman she is.* I quickly checked my thoughts; it caught me off guard. *How dare I think of my friend's mother that way.* Maybe I was becoming a man in my mind, a little too early. If I was supposed to be keeping the Law as of tomorrow, I had better start practising.

***

Yeshua and I spent the day wandering through the vineyard and checking out the area in and around Bethany. We talked and talked. I asked him if he wanted to go to Jerusalem, but to my surprise, he said that he was fine with waiting until tomorrow. He wanted to spend the day with me.

During our discussions, I asked him about some of the things he said when I was in Nazareth. I expressed my concerns about how what he said seemed to contradict our scriptures.

"I don't see how loving our enemy is opposite to the Law of God. Love reaches out to everyone. It is inclusive. God loves everyone, including the Romans, and so should we," Yeshua said.

I shook my head in disagreement.

"Lazarus, what good does it do to only love those who love you? Truly, if you want to be like God, you must love those who have hurt you or hate you. I'm not talking in opposition to the commandments; rather I'm talking about taking the understanding of them beyond what is there on the surface."

I ran my hands through my hair and said, "I don't really understand. Where do you get this teaching? Is that what you are taught in the north?"

He smiled, "No, I received it from my Father, the one who loves us all."

"Come on Yeshua. You can't go around calling God your father. That is simply stupid and you could get yourself in very serious trouble. You have to stop talking like that," I admonished him.

He went silent.

Oops, I thought, *I've pushed him too much.*

We walked to the top of the hill behind Bethany. It was quite a walk up, but it was worth the view. It was a higher hill than the small vineyard hill behind our home. We stood in silence for some time. It was not a holy silence; we had a disagreement, and I searched for the words to break the uncomfortableness between us. However, Yeshua spoke first.

"I know the way I speak of God seems strange to you Lazarus, but someday you will understand."

"I hope so because right now I don't understand."

That is pretty much how we left the discussion. We were still friends of course, but we approached God differently. I told him I would pray for him. Yeshua just smiled at me as if he knew something I did not.

***

The next morning, I woke with the sun shining on my face. It took a few minutes for me to fully wake. When I did, my nerves instantly took over and I trembled. *This is the day*, I thought to myself, *Adonai, Adonai, please be with me.* I continued to pray until I heard someone outside my room. "Yeshua?" I said.

"No, it's your father, my young man. Yom huledet sameach, Eleazar," he said. "I'd like you to come downstairs."

Everyone had gathered in the living area to wait for me. They greeted me with hugs, Happy Birthday wishes until my father cleared his throat, and everyone stood still in all seriousness.

"Lazarus, we understand what a special day this is for you, and how excited you are. I also know that you will be missing someone very important in your life; your mother."

I nodded and tried to contain my emotions.

"You should know that your mother is with you today," Abba said, "Martha?"

Martha walked out from behind Yosef and Myriam carrying a beautifully woven white and blue prayer shawl.

"Your mother completed your prayer shawl before she died. This is her gift to you," he said as my sisters unfolded the shawl.

"I wanted you to see this before I placed it across your shoulders at the Temple," my father said.

By this time the tears were flowing. I was officially an adult in our faith today, but at that moment, I cried like a baby. My father held me. I looked around to see that I was not the only one in tears. Both my sisters, still holding the shawl, threw their arms around me.

*　*　*

Yosef appreciated being able to use the cart to go to Jerusalem. The women loaded the cart with food and cushions for the celebration after my ceremony. Our cart was small; we used it in our vineyard to carry the ripened grapes down to the winery barn. Today it was perfect for our travelling needs.

The women took turns riding with Yosef on the cart. We did not have a mule, so Yeshua and I pulled the cart down to the Temple. We laughed and enjoyed the short trip. Happy, with my nerves calmed, joy filled my heart.

The ceremony was full of meaning for me, and I managed to keep a smile on my face, as my father put my mother's prayer shawl on my shoulders. I was glad that he had presented it to me before we left for the Temple.

The moment I stood before the crowd, that gathered to hear me proclaim the Scripture passage, I felt Adonai's presence and His closeness. Before I began to read, I scanned the faces in the room; my eyes met Yeshua's. He smiled and nodded to me. I read with a surety that surprised me.

E. Ann McIntyre

Chapter 10 "Todah, Abba"

The reception was boisterous with plenty of dancing, singing, and clapping. I stood in the middle as the men danced around me, as they did I copied their movements, swaying back and forth. The women and girls watched from the sides of the room. Under the Law, they could not dance with the men. However, they could clap and sing.

At one point during the festive dancing, I could see Myriam, Yeshua's mother, trying to get his attention. I moved over to his side of the circle and spoke to him in a loud voice so he could hear me above the noise, "You mother wants you!"

He looked over at her and immediately left the circle of dancers. I watched him until he disappeared out the door. The dancing and singing continued for another few minutes until my father shouted that it was time to eat.

My sister Martha rushed to my side and said, "Yosef has taken ill. Yeshua and Myriam took him on the cart to the Zebedee house. Yeshua asked if you would come."

Amid my own celebration, torn as to what to do, I asked Abba. When my father heard about Yosef's sudden illness, he told me to go. He and the girls would stay with our guests for a little while longer.

***

I ran through the Temple's outer court to the street; it seemed to take forever to get to the Zebedee house, even though it was only a ten-minute walk. I could not get there fast enough. When I got to the house, the cart was beside the door, which was slightly ajar. I knocked on it. Yeshua came to the door and looked through the narrow opening. Tears were streaming down his face. He motioned me in.

Myriam was kneeling down on the floor cradling her husband's head in her lap. I wasn't sure if Yosef was alive or dead. He looked ashen, but as I looked carefully, I could see his chest rise and fall with each slow shallow breath. He was dying.

Yeshua walked past me and knelt beside his mother. He held her as she held Yosef. I felt that I was an intruder into their very private moment. I turned to leave.

"Please stay, Lazarus. I need you," Yeshua said softly, "Would you pray the twenty-third psalm for us?"

I began,

"The Lord is my shepherd, I shall not want.
He makes me lie down in green pastures;
He leads me beside still waters;
He restores my soul
He leads me in right paths for his name's sake
Even though I walk through the darkest valley."

My voice began to quiver on the words. A strong and gentle voice came from behind me, it was my father, and he picked up the words of the psalm and continued for me.

"No evil do I fear for you are there with your rod and your staff,
with these, you give me comfort."

E. Ann McIntyre

I sat next to Yeshua, as Yosef's breathing grew even shallower, and then as Myriam held him in her arms, Yosef breathed his last. Myriam leaned over her husband's body, weeping, kissing, and holding him for a few more minutes. We prayed silently. Myriam moved back and allowed Yeshua a moment with Yosef's body.

Yeshua kissed Yosef's forehead, and with tears pouring down his face whispered, "Todah, Abba." [Thank you, Father].

That was the first time in my hearing that Yeshua called Yosef "*Father*".

Myriam spoke to my father, "We have nowhere to lay him here in Jerusalem. Do you know of a place?"

My father knew it was impossible for them to take Yosef's body back to Nazareth.

"Myriam, do not worry about that, you can place him in my family's tomb just outside of Bethany."

"Thank you," Myriam replied as she wiped her eyes.

Martha asked Myriam if she could help her prepare Yosef's body for burial. This was what the women did in our custom. Myriam nodded.

"We will need some oil, spices, and a burial cloth," Myriam said.

"I will go get those things for you," Father said.

"Yeshua, do you have some coins to give Boethius?" Myriam asked.

"Please, let me buy them for you," Father said to her.

"Thank you. You all are too kind," she said.

Father left for the market.

The house was empty except for us; the Zebedee family was not in Jerusalem at that time. I touched

Yeshua on the shoulder and suggested that we could go to the roof to pray while the women made the preparations. He nodded.

We climbed the stairs in silence. I thought we might sit in the middle of the roof, as we had done during Passover, to pray, however, Yeshua walked to the half wall at the roof's edge. He leaned with both hands on the top edge of the wall. He lifted his eyes to the Temple, and spoke, at first in a whisper, but then in a loud pleading voice.

"Why now? Why now? You must know that I still need him," he said. "I can't do this without him. He is my rock, my protector. Who will care for us? Who will care for Mother? Please, please bring him back to me. I know you can."

I stood back a few feet from Yeshua as he made his impossible petition to God. I remembered my own grief and struggle with God when my mother died. Now, my friend was going through the same thing. I felt helpless.

He turned around and faced in my direction, but he wasn't looking at me. He held his hands to his face and sunk down the wall to a sitting position on the roof with his knees pulled up to his chest. His body shook with his sobs.

I walked over and sat down beside him. I put my hand on his shoulder. He looked up at me. He was pale and drawn; something within him had changed. The boy I played with in the mud two months ago was gone. In his eyes, I saw someone different. In his grief, Yeshua had suddenly become a man.

Yeshua took a deep breath, stretched out his legs and said, "Lazarus, you are my closest friend. I need

E. Ann McIntyre

to tell you something. Something I need you to know, but you cannot tell anyone, including your father.

I nodded. I wasn't sure what he was about to tell me. I waited as he gathered his thoughts.

"I have already told you that Yosef is not my father. My mother conceived me before she and Yosef came to live together as husband and wife. She did not know any man when she conceived me. She was a virgin. An angel from God visited her. The angel told her that the power of the Most High would come upon her, and she would conceive a son, who would be called the Son of the Most High."

I sat back hard against the stonewall cracking my head against it as I did so. "What?" I said almost involuntarily. He nodded.

This is blasphemy. He cannot speak like this.

"I know how this must sound but please hear me out," Yeshua said as he wiped the remaining tears from his face.

He went on to tell me about a visit his mother had made to her cousin Elizabeth, who had conceived a child even though she was way past childbearing age. He spoke of Yosef wanting to divorce his mother quietly rather than have her stoned, however, after an encounter with an angel in a dream; he took Myriam as his wife.

My head was dizzy with all this impossible information. There was more.

Yeshua told me of his parents travelling to Bethlehem, because of Caesar Augustus's census decree the year we were both born. He spoke of shepherds visiting him after he was born because singing angels had declared that the Messiah had been born in a stable in Bethlehem, the City of David.

Is he saying he is the Messiah? Adonai... please stop him.

He told me of a star in the sky, which led three wise men from the east to the family's stable residence. They brought gold, frankincense, and myrrh for him. These gifts financed a six-year stay in Egypt because Herod sought to kill him. Instead, Herod killed all the boys under three in Bethlehem.

I was stunned. I thought my friend had gone mad. "Yeshua, Yeshua, please stop this. You are talking as though you are mad. I can't listen to this any longer." I immediately left the roof and flopped on a cot in the Upper Room.

I began to weep for him; *he is so grieved by Yosef's death that he has become delusional.* I prayed my heart out to God for him. I had to figure out how to get him help, although I promised not to tell anyone what he just told me, I thought that there must be some way I could alert my father to Yeshua's condition, so he could help him. Perhaps there were demons inside Yeshua, and my father, as the High Priest, could drive them out.

I closed my eyes in prayer and unwittingly fell asleep. The next thing I knew my father was standing over me.

"Where is Yeshua?" he asked. I pointed to the roof.

"I need to speak with him. It is too late today to take Yosef's body to Bethany, but we should be prepared to go first thing in the morning."

I nodded.

"Abba"

"Yes, son."

"Yeshua is not well."

E. Ann McIntyre

"He is in shock and in grief over the loss of his father. You remember what you went through when your mother died."

"It's more than that. It is deeper. I don't know how to explain it. Maybe he'll talk to you and you can see what I'm talking about," I said, "Abba, I'm worried about him."

"Son, if you're that concerned, I'll see if I can get him to open up to me."

"Thank you Abba, I hope he does."

My father went up to the roof to talk to Yeshua. They were up there together for a couple of hours. It was dark before they finally came down. Yeshua nodded to me as he continued downstairs to join his mother. Father came and sat beside me.

"Yeshua is going through a very difficult time son. He is worried about a number of things right now. He told me that Myriam is not the mother of the older children in the family. I'm not sure if you are aware, Lazarus, but James, Yossi, and Jude are not therefore obliged to support Myriam and Yeshua. James will inherit the house and Yosef's business. Yeshua will have to find a way to support both he and his mother. He is thirteen, and that is an awful burden for him to carry at his age. He said that he and his mother can move in with his grandmother Anna, but he will either have to form a partnership with his brothers, and get paid whatever is left over, or go into business for himself."

I sat there trying to comprehend my friend's immediate future. I had no idea he would face such difficulties. I felt bad for leaving him so suddenly on the roof. I was not the friend I should have been during his time of grief.

I got up and we went downstairs to have some supper. The women had moved Yosef's body into an adjoining room and prepared for burial. Martha had brought some of the food from my reception to the house for our supper.

I sat next to Yeshua and whispered an apology to him for my abrupt departure from the roof. He told me all was well, he understood my dilemma over his story.

After supper, we said the prayers for the sorrowful, and then we turned in for the night. Tomorrow we would rise early to make the sad walk to the Bethany burial ground.

***

Our small funeral processed out of Jerusalem very early in the morning, before sunrise. The late fall air was cool but not cold. Yeshua and I pulled the cart with Yosef's shrouded body uphill all the way to Bethany's burial grounds on the outskirts of town.

Myriam walked with my father, my sisters followed behind them. It was a quiet, respectful journey. Yeshua and I stopped at the entrance to the burial grounds, while father and Martha went ahead to prepare a shelf on which to lay Yosef's body. We waited a few minutes. There were no tears, only quiet grieving. Father came to the tomb entrance and waved us forward.

The three of us carried the body and placed it gently on the rock shelf in the tomb. I shuddered slightly; we had buried mother nearby. We left the sepulchre in silence.

E. Ann McIntyre

Yeshua and I pushed the rock in its place in front of the tomb. We picked up the cart handles and turned toward Bethany. Yeshua and his mother stayed with us that night, before going back to Nazareth the next day.

Chapter 11 Son of Who?

We walked with Yeshua and Myriam to the town center and to the waiting caravan that my father had arranged to take them back to Nazareth. Martha had acquired black clothing, suitable for a widow, for Myriam. She would wear black for the rest of her life unless she re-married.

As we bid them farewell, Yeshua told me he would continue to come to Jerusalem for as many of the feasts each year as he could. That gave me hope that we would see each other regularly. We wished them "Shalom" as they departed.

Father gathered us together for the walk home. "They will be all right, Yeshua has a good head on his shoulders, and he will find a way to take care of his mother and himself."

"Abba, why is Yeshua so sad?" Miriam asked.

Father and I looked at each other in complete astonishment. Apparently, my sister had not paid attention to what had transpired over the last two days.

Father cleared his throat and said to Miriam. "Yosef was Yeshua's father and he just died, that's why Yeshua is sad, just as you were sad when your mother died."

Miriam shook her head, "No Abba, Yosef wasn't Yeshua's father. He just took care of him."

I gasped and thought, *Has Miriam been listening in to my conversations with Yeshua?* I waited to see what else was going to come out of her mouth.

"Well now, is that so?" my father said.

Miriam nodded.

"Who is Yeshua's father?" he asked my youngest sister.

I closed my eyes in anticipation of the answer.

"Adonai!" she said.

My Father, the High Priest, the defender and protector of our Jewish faith took a deep breath, knelt down to Miriam's eye level and said softly, "Who told you that?"

"Yeshua," she whispered.

Father, still kneeling, looked up at me and asked, "Have you heard any of this kind of talk from Yeshua, Lazarus?"

I gulped, "Yes Abba, I have."

My father's face turned beet-red. "We will continue this discussion at home," Father said as he rushed us along the road to our house.

***

We sat on the cushions in our living area, with Father sitting in front of the three of us. I was in the middle, the hot seat. Father looked at me and said as gently as he could under the circumstances, "Lazarus, tell me exactly what Yeshua said to you about his relationship with God, and when did he say it?"

"Well, I first caught reference to his thinking when we were praying on the roof of the Zebedee house during Passover; he called God "*my father*". I did question what he said but he never really explained his words to me."

"What else did he say?" Father asked.

"You remember what he said to his mother when we found him in the temple?"

"Yes, I do."

"It was after that up in the vineyard that he told me that Yosef was not his father, but he didn't say at that point who was."

"So, did he ever actually tell you that God was his father?"

I nodded, "Yes, yesterday when we were up on the roof. He told me the story of how he came to be."

"Perhaps son you and I should go for a walk in the vineyard."

We left my sisters in the house, disappointed I'm sure, not to be able to hear the whole story.

Father rubbed his beard frequently as we walked through the vineyard while I recalled Yeshua's words about angels, "*Son of the Most High*", dreams, shepherds, a star, and wise men. It was Yeshua's words, "*Son of the Most High*", that caught my father's attention.

"Indeed, by saying that he implied that he is the "Son of God", and that is blasphemy."

"I know. That is why, on several occasions, I told him to stop talking like that and why I left him on the roof yesterday, I just couldn't listen to him anymore."

"You were right to do that," my father said.

I felt the need to ask my father a question, to confirm one of the things Yeshua told me. I mean, everybody can see an unusual star in the sky, can they not?

"Was there a strange star in the sky the year I was born?" I asked him.

E. Ann McIntyre

"Yes, there was. I remember it appeared a couple of months before you were born. It was mainly over the eastern part of the sky. It stayed there for a few years before it disappeared. You know, it probably appeared about the time of Yeshua's birth."

Well at least that part of Yeshua's story is true, I thought to myself.

"Father, he also mentioned that Herod ordered the killing of male children under two years old in Bethlehem. His family escaped to Egypt because an angel told Yosef in a dream about the threat to Yeshua. Did that happen?" I asked.

"Yes son, it did. My father was particularly affected because he performed the circumcision and Dedication ceremony for those children."

"None of these parts of the story concern me. Those things you mentioned are known to have taken place. What does concern me is the first part of the story. Yeshua's claim, of an angel of God visiting his mother and that she conceived from God. That is the problem."

My father continued to walk, pondering what to do. I walked with him and waited. The High Priest had obligations, a duty to uphold the teachings of our faith and to ensure that all the people of Israel held to those teachings.

"I will go to Nazareth to talk to Yeshua. I will wait a couple of months to allow him to get their lives settled after Yosef's death."

"What will you do Father?"

"The Law is strict in cases like this. I will issue a warning to him to stop speaking of these things. He must agree. If he does, that is fine. I will not need to pursue the matter any further. However, if he refuses to cease, he puts both himself and possibly his mother at grave risk. I would have to bring both of them to the Sanhedrin to face the charge of blasphemy."

I cringed. I knew what that meant. If found guilty they would be sentenced to death by stoning. I also knew that Yeshua was aware of this and that is why he commanded that I not tell my father. I felt as though I had betrayed him.

***

It was after the Festival of Lights when Father decided to go to Nazareth. The middle of winter was not an ideal time to travel. Snow, especially in the highlands of the Northern provinces, was possible. Caravans still went between the cities but there could be weather-related delays en route. The usual two and half to three-day journey could wind up taking longer.

Father booked a caravan and was advised to bring as much warm clothing and blankets with him as he could. Martha was more than up to the challenge of seeing to Father's comfort. We walked with Father to the caravan where Martha piled the blankets on him. The weather in Bethany that week had been cool and rainy, which did not bode well for the journey into the northern hills.

Before he departed, Father gave me instruction on filling the orders he had for wine from the governor's palace, including how much I should receive in payment, so they could not try to cheat me. He also advised me to cut plenty of wood, so Martha could keep the house warm.

I wished him "Shalom", and we waved good-bye as the caravan disappeared. I lingered on the

E. Ann McIntyre

road; I wanted to go with him but this was something on which he had to engage Yeshua privately.

***

During the winter months, I did not sleep in my room on the roof because the warmth from the fire in the hearth did not reach up there. I usually slept in the living area but with Father gone, I slept in his room.

For the next few nights, my sleep was very restless. I kept having nightmares about Yeshua and my father, with their meeting not going well. I even dreamt that Yeshua got stoned. That dream scared me and I woke up shaking.

At the end of the first week of Father's absence, we were coping quite well. Martha told me I was a good provider and did everything as Father would do it. That pleased me and I felt very grown up.

One afternoon I came home from the Temple to find my sisters crying. I had no idea what had happened until Martha showed me a letter. It was from Father.

"*Just as my return trip began there was an accident with the caravan cart. A wheel came off it, throwing me out on to the road and into a rocky ditch. My right leg was broken in the fall. I was in a lot of pain. The caravan drivers carried me back to Nazareth. I am in the care of Yeshua, Myriam, and Anna. Yeshua got a Greek physician from Sepphoris who bound my leg. The physician told me it would be a couple of months before I could even try to walk again. I am still experiencing pain but it's not as bad as when the bone broke.*"

He ended the letter by telling us he did not know when he could return to Bethany. It was difficult to get a caravan that was willing to take someone who could not walk.

We were in shock. I was not sure what to do. Go to Nazareth myself and bring him home or stay with my sisters and wait? Martha wanted me to stay. She needed me to help take care of everything. Miriam was afraid something might happen to me too if I went off in the winter to Nazareth. We decided that as long as Father was cared for in Nazareth he would be fine and would come home when he was able.

I wrote Father a note to tell him that we would wait for his return. We wished him well. I also sent our thanks to Yeshua, Myriam, and Anna for taking care of my father. I told Father that all was well with us.

***

It was four days after I sent my letter to my father via a caravan. We had just finished supper when I heard footsteps outside our door. As I reached for the door, it opened in my hand. Standing in the entrance was my father.

Cheers and cries of surprise greeted him. We nearly knocked him down. Suddenly I became conscious of his broken leg and tried to help him to his cot. He waved me off.

"Look, look, I'm fine. The leg isn't broken anymore," he said.

"How is that possible, Abba, didn't the physician tell you it would take months to heal?" I said.

"Yes, he did say that. However, I have a story for you. Come, my family, sit with me."

E. Ann McIntyre

We settled around him as he recounted for us what happened to him in Nazareth.

"It was about three days after the accident and I was still in considerable pain. Myriam had set me up in the living area for sleeping, but I was having difficulty getting to sleep with the pain in my leg. Myriam and Anna had gone to bed. Yeshua was sitting with me. I had had my talk with him. So we were on good terms," my father said with a smile.

"Yeshua suggested that we say our Evening Prayer. When we finished, Yeshua asked me if I would like him to heal my leg. I was a little taken aback, to say the least. I asked him how he could possibly do that. Had he ever healed anyone before? He said "no". Then he whispered to me that his father had commanded him to heal me. I nearly lost my temper with him. However, before I could say or do anything, Yeshua laid his hands on my leg, closed his eyes and prayed. His hands grew warm on my flesh, a sudden surge of warmth went through my entire body, and my leg no longer hurt. Yeshua opened his eyes, looked at me, and said, "Your leg is healed." It was. I could move it. Yeshua helped me to my feet. I was stunned."

"Yeshua then said to me, "I'll make a deal with you. You don't tell anybody except your family about this and I won't tell anyone who my father is as long as you are the High Priest." I honestly did not know what to say. He had done something that some would call a miracle. I did not know what to believe about him. I told him that God gifted certain people as healers and some people as prophets who speak in God's name but none of them ever claimed to be the "Son of God". I was still firm with him. I told him I could help him understand this gift. He agreed. So when he comes here for the festivals, the two of us will meet to discuss his gift and how he can discern who should be healed."

After my sisters went to bed, Father took me aside and told me more of what had transpired in Nazareth. The day after his healing Yeshua went to Sepphoris to secure a caravan going to Jerusalem for my father. While he was gone, my father took the opportunity to ask Myriam more about Yeshua. Father told me she was tight-lipped about Yeshua's patrimony; he did not press her. She did tell him that Yeshua had never healed anyone before. Myriam was pleased that my father was prepared to take thirteen-year-old Yeshua under his spiritual guidance.

"I told Myriam that it was fortunate that I was the one to speak to Yeshua about how he expressed his relationship with God. I told her that my successor, Yosef Caiaphas, would not be quite so lenient."

Chapter 12 Eleazar of the Priestly Line of Aaron

My fourteenth year was an intense year of preparation for assuming my role as a priest. I spent the six months from Passover to Sukkot at the Temple. I thought it was to be a year of learning more rituals and laws. However, under the guidance of Master Yosef of Arimathea, it was a time of tremendous spiritual growth, filled with a great deal of soul searching and discernment. Yosef called it a journey into the desert without actually going there. Yosef told me that not all descendants of Aaron were priests. This was a time for me to discern that the life of a priest was truly my calling.

During festivals, I observed a regime of strict silence and fasting. I did not have too much difficulty with the silence, but all I could think about was eating. Master Yosef would laugh at me because my stomach made more noise than my tongue did.

During those six months, I only saw my sisters when they came to the Temple for feast days. I saw my father regularly as he was there for his duties. He would bring news from home and even mentioned that he had regular meetings with Yeshua; apparently, he was so eager to learn from my father's wisdom that he came to the house at least once a month even if there wasn't a feast. I saw Yeshua during the festivals, but because I was in strict silence, I couldn't talk to him. He would just smile and wave at me. I was looking forward to Sukkot – my freedom festival, after which I could go home to a normal life.

* * *

The time finally came when, at fifteen, I was old enough to assume my priestly duties in the Temple. Martha was busy making my special robes. She started her work on my robes months before I needed them. Martha measured me and then disappeared into her room, forbidding me to peek. I told her that the robes should be made with the finest material money could buy. All the while Father insisted that I could not outshine the High Priest.

"Don't worry, Abba, he won't," Martha assured him.

My father would consecrate me after Sukkot, a week after my fifteenth birthday. A month before my consecration as a priest, Yeshua arrived for his monthly meeting with my father. He was eager to discuss my upcoming weeklong special service. During the ritual, I was to have someone put the phylactery on me; I asked Yeshua if he would do the honours. He happily accepted.

A few days before my consecration, the Zebedee family arrived to announce a new addition. Zebedee made the formal request to my father to perform the circumcision and Dedication ceremony for their newborn. The ceremony would take place after my installation, so Father invited me to participate in the ritual, my first formal ritual as a priest. I was delighted.

My consecration days finally came, with many of my friends and fellow students in attendance, as was the Sanhedrin. I was nervous but not overly so. I had been preparing for the moment since I was six years old. I felt at peace and joyful.

Father prayed the Priestly Blessing over me, performed the ritual sacrifice for my sins and smeared the blood on my hands. It was a ritual passed down through the ages; a new priest is smeared with blood, the High Priest is anointed with oil. Father sent me off to pray. The next day I came back for more purification and was sent off to pray again. This continued until the final day when I received my priestly robes. Martha carried them in part way as she could not cross into the sanctuary. Yeshua met her there and carried them to my father who prayed his blessing over them. Both my father and Yeshua helped me put them on. I glanced over at the Court of the Women and bowed thankfully in Martha's direction. The robes were beautiful. I saw Martha wipe her eyes.

Yeshua fitted the Phylacteries on me. They had belonged to my grandfather Simeon. I was so pleased that my father had saved them for me. It was an honor to be entrusted with them.

Thus began my life as a priest. I would be fully vested in my priestly role when I reached the age of twenty. At twenty, I would be eligible to sit on the Sanhedrin. It would be at least another ten years before the Roman Governor would consider me for the position of High Priest.

***

The day after my final ceremony, baby bar Zebedee was eight days old. It was now time to assist my father in my first ritual as priest. The Zebedee family and extended family gathered at the Temple. My father met them at the top step just outside the altar area. Salome held her son in her arms. Before I took the child, my father asked Zebedee the ritual question.

"What do you name this child?"

"He is to be called John," Zebedee replied.

I took the child from his mother and followed my father to the altar. The men followed us. The women went to their court to watch at a distance. I thought my father was going to perform the circumcision but he handed me the knife. He rested his hand on mine to steady it. I cut the skin quickly. Baby John cried but not too much. My father prayed the invocation declaring John bar Zebedee a member of God's chosen people united through the covenant God had made with our Father Abraham.

I held the baby up high for all to see then I lowered him, intending to put him in the arms of his father Zebedee, but somehow baby John wound up in the arms of his cousin Yeshua.

Yeshua cradled his new cousin gently in his arms, with his finger held firmly in John's closed left fist; the baby's right fist was mightily punching Yeshua's hand, who cooed, "A Son of Thunder are you?" The name stuck. Yeshua cuddled the child declaring they would be very good friends, to which James bar Zebedee declared, "Hey, he's my brother."

Yeshua handed the baby over to his elder brother. I don't think Zebedee got his son back that

E. Ann McIntyre

day. A new baby turns even the most stoic man into mush.

***

The reception was held at the Zebedee house, a place that was becoming my second Jerusalem home. My sisters were busy helping Myriam of Nazareth with the serving. I was surprised to see even my sister Miriam pitching in. I guessed that Martha had been encouraging her to get involved in the service of hospitality.

Salome appeared with the baby after attending to his needs. Yeshua was sitting on the floor legs flat out with a cushion in his lap ready to receive young John. Salome laughed and placed the baby with his new babysitter - Yeshua was delighted.

"You know, Yeshua, you should be making arrangements with one of Nazareth's finest young ladies so you can have your own children." my father said.

Yeshua laughed and said, "I don't think there are any unattached young women in Nazareth. There is a young Roman girl in Sepphoris I like. I do work for her father."

"A Roman!" my father said, "You can't married a Roman!"

"Why not?" Yeshua said, "Is there a Law against that?"

Now, I knew Yeshua was baiting my father just to get a reaction. He succeeded.

"Yeshua, stop that," his mother said, "You know better."

Yeshua nodded and continued to play with the baby's hands. "Well, what about Lazarus? Have you arranged a contract for him yet?"

"No, but that is next on my list for him," my father said, "I can't let our line from Aaron get too thin you know."

My jaw dropped, "Father! I don't have time for courting."

"Oh you will my son, you will make the time," my father said with a grin on his face.

I hated that kind of conversation, especially because I was the last in a line of High Priests. The pressure to continue the line would be on me from now on. I wished I at least knew a girl who might be interested in me.

I decided to switch the focus back on Yeshua, "So, Yeshua, you are of the line of David, aren't you?"

He nodded.

"So aren't you concerned that perhaps your line might produce the Messiah? If you don't get married that wouldn't happen," I told him.

"Maybe the Messiah has already come... and I am he?" Yeshua said matter-of-factly.

That brought hoots and laughter from everyone in the room with the exception of my father.

"Yeshua, don't even joke about that. The coming of the Messiah is a serious matter."

My father just sat there shaking his head mumbling to himself, "All I want in my old age is a grandson and somehow we got to the coming of the Messiah!"

During the conversation, I took a glance at Yeshua's mother. She was not laughing. She instead

E. Ann McIntyre

had a serious look of concern on her face. I remembered the words Yeshua used when he described his birth, *"Son of the Most High"* I shivered.

***

I settled into my life as a priest doing my duties at the Temple. As I neared the age of twenty, Father fretted over my marital status. Oh, he attempted to indulge my fancy with a parade of potential young brides, but to no avail. There was always a problem. Either I was unsuitable or she was. I think Father was growing tired of the whole business of trying to marry off his children, with first Martha's resistance, and then my apparent lack of suitable partners. Miriam was his only hope for descendants.

Things weren't much better in the north. Yeshua was single too. He claimed he was too busy trying to establish his own business so he could better support his mother. Maybe his excuse was better than mine.

We still got together for festival celebrations but he no longer sought the counsel of my father. Father had brought him along the path to spiritual independence. Yeshua hadn't healed anyone besides my father that I knew of, still, I thought that being able to heal was an amazing gift.

My father was getting older and at the age of forty, he felt it was time to step aside as High Priest. He looked forward to spending more time in the vineyard. That was the year I turned twenty and became a fully vested priest.

The Roman Governor Valerius Gratus appointed Yosef Caiaphas as High Priest. I attended his elaborate installation and anointing ceremony. Under

High Priest Caiaphas, the rules and regulations for priests were strictly enforced. My father had warned me to expect this tightening of the interpretation of the Law, so I was prepared. Caiaphas was also concerned about the relationship between the Romans and the temple officials. He was determined to keep things in order. The political tensions in the region were increasing. So far, Jerusalem had remained peaceful; however, word had come to the Temple that a serious situation had developed in the northern region of the country, which was under the control of Herod. Clashes between the Zealots and the Roman army were becoming more frequent.

Chapter 13 Yeshua's World

One summer Yeshua invited me to come north for a visit. I hadn't been there since I was twelve, so the idea of taking time to visit him was very exciting. Yeshua wanted to take me around his home and see where he worked. He planned a visit with the Zebedee family in Capernaum; perhaps we could go fishing.

It was the first time I ventured out of the Jerusalem area on my own. I never had much need to go anywhere, so a visit with my friend was a welcome distraction from Temple duties. The journey was relaxing. I took the same route as when I went with my family those many years ago. We travelled out to the great sea and then the caravan travelled northeast. The reason for taking what might appear to be the long way to Galilee was that going directly north from Jerusalem would take us through Samaria; Jews rarely ventured through that territory, because the Samaritans were not true Jews.

Yeshua met me at the same place where he had met us before. He laughed and said that the caravans always stop there. The scenery was pretty much the same with one very disturbing exception; off in the distance, I could see crosses, a lot of them. The Romans crucified rebels outside of Jerusalem too, but I had never seen so many crosses at once.

Yeshua saw me looking at them. "The Zealots tried to storm the Roman barracks. They didn't succeed. It was awful. It affected everyone here, either by sheer fear or by losing a family member. There were four men from Nazareth killed. Two of them were not even involved in the raid. The soldiers just came and took them."

"How did you escape?" I asked him.

"Well, the commander was Gaius Marius, the Centurion who had supper with us, remember?"

I nodded.

"He stood in front of our home and never let any of the soldiers near our door," Yeshua said.

"He remembered too," I said.

"Yes, he did. He only spoke to me once and that was to tell me to stay out of sight."

"What about your brothers?"

"They were in Sepphoris. The Romans never went there. They hunted the Zealots down in the small towns and in the hills.

"When did this happen?"

"Two weeks ago. It's still pretty raw. People are still in shock," Yeshua said.

As we climbed the hill to Yeshua's home, I glanced over my shoulder at the crosses. This is exactly what worried High Priest Caiaphas. I could see now that his concern was justified.

***

The welcome to the home of Yeshua and his mother was wonderful. Myriam had prepared a scrumptious dinner for me and we talked late into the evening. Myriam's mother Anna had passed away a few years prior, leaving the house to her grandson. They also kept Anna's sheep because Myriam used

E. Ann McIntyre

their wool for her own creations on the loom. Yeshua worked in Sepphoris most days except on the Sabbath. He was making a good income, enough to keep them both comfortable.

After Myriam turned in for the night, Yeshua and I went outside on the roof to talk. During Yeshua's visits to Jerusalem, we were so busy with the festivals that we really did not get much opportunity to talk as we had when we were younger. On my first night in Nazareth, we decided we had some catching up to do.

We were both twenty-five, and each of us still had one living parent. For Yeshua, the death of Yosef had put him in the awkward place of having to support both himself and his mother when he was only thirteen. He had to grow up fast. My path to maturity was a little slower I suppose, as my father still provided for our family. Martha was the one who had to assume the adult role of "mother" to our household.

As we sat on the roof under the stars, we commiserated about the curves life had thrown at us. One thing became clear during our conversation; Yeshua was still determined to become a wandering rabbi. I also got some insight into the relationship between him and my father.

"When I told Boethius that I wanted to be a rabbi who goes out to the people to teach them about God, he told me about an ancient way of teaching by telling parables," he said.

"What are parables?" I asked him.

"They are stories you put together about everyday things and events that people experience in their lives. These stories incorporate a special teaching about God," Yeshua said.

"Have you composed any parables?"

"A few. I'll tell you one and see if you get its meaning."

"Okay, I'm listening."

Yeshua got up and repositioned himself to sit directly across from me. He took the lantern off the shelf and put it between us like it was a campfire. He sat cross-legged, hands folded, and fingers to his mouth. Then he began to teach me in the manner my father had taught him.

"There was a man, a Jew, who was attacked by some thugs. They beat him, stole his money and left him for dead on the side of the road. By and by, a rabbi came along and saw the man, looked at him and said to him, "Be well" but did nothing to help him. Next, a priest from the Temple came along, he saw the man, but he crossed to the other side of the road so he didn't have to walk by the man."

"Oh sure, make the priest a bad guy," I said.

Yeshua held up his hand and continued, "Next a Samaritan came along and took pity on the man. He cleaned his wounds, picked the man up and took him to an inn. There he gave the innkeeper enough money to care for the man until he was well."

"Which of these is righteous in the sight of God?" Yeshua asked.

I sat there staring at Yeshua as he prompted me to answer his question.

"Okay, in this story the Samaritan is the righteous one. But you're going to have to change that parable because nobody will accept that a Samaritan is godlier than a rabbi or a priest," I said.

"Are you sure about that?" Yeshua asked me.

E. Ann McIntyre

"Yes, I am sure. Did you tell my father that one?" I asked him.

"Not yet, but when I do I will use "High Priest" instead of "priest," Yeshua said with a smile.

"Oh that will go over well," I said.

I was pleased Yeshua had let me in on his plans and used me to practice his teaching style.

**

The next morning, Yeshua and I met on the roof for Morning Prayer. I had finally mastered the art of getting up early to pray. Yeshua was impressed to find me sitting on the roof waiting for him before sunrise.

"Well, this is a surprise, I don't have to wake you up," he said with a smile.

"I enjoy getting up in the early mornings now, it has become a habit," I said.

After we finished our prayer, Yeshua asked, "Do you have anything else to wear besides priestly robes?"

Surprised, I said, "No I don't, why do you ask?"

"Well, you might want to dress down somewhat. You are not in the Temple, so do you really need to wear such formal attire while you are here?" he asked.

I felt offended, I could feel my face getting red, but since it came from Yeshua, I tried to brush off the comment.

"As a priest, I'm expected to wear my priestly garments all the time no matter where I am," I informed him. He did not push the issue of my attire any further.

After prayers but before breakfast we had a chore to do; to put the sheep out to pasture and let their guard donkeys stand with them. Old Jenny and young Jenny were still doing a fine job of taking care of the small herd of sheep, a fact that I still found amusing.

Myriam had breakfast ready for us when we finished up with the sheep. As we ate, I couldn't help but notice just how much Miriam and Yeshua looked alike. Her fine feminine features graced her face with her large brown almond shaped eyes adding to the beauty I had noticed when I was young. Yeshua's face was like hers only with a strong masculine outline. Their eyes were identical. Miriam's hair was a mixture of dark brown and grey, at least from what I could see from under her black headdress. Yeshua's equally dark brown hair was two inches beyond shoulder length and his full beard had touches of grey in it, making him look older and wiser than his actual years.

I kept my black hair short with the side curls beside my face. My well-trimmed beard came to a point at my chin. Only the High Priest could have a full long beard. I maintained the look of a priest in every aspect of my appearance.

Yeshua walked everywhere he went, rarely taking a caravan cart. After breakfast, it was time to take a three-mile stroll to the neighbouring city of Sepphoris, where Yeshua made his living. I was surprised at the size of the city and the ethnicity of its people. There were Romans of course, Greeks, Jews, and Asians, all intermingling without much concern. Yeshua said that the Romans were rebuilding the city after a massive earthquake a number of years ago. That rebuilding effort kept artisans like him busy. Herod Antipas had made Sepphoris the capital of

Galilee, so it was a place of much commerce, political activity, and culture. A theatre supported the Greeks in their production of plays. We watched a rehearsal for a while; although we could see the thespians, we couldn't hear them from our vantage point.

Yeshua showed me a few of the buildings he and his brothers had constructed. One of the buildings was a large villa. They had completed their work on the project but there was still work going on inside. Yeshua took me in to watch the tile painter as he designed a beautiful mosaic on the floor.

"I could never walk on that floor, it is far too beautiful," I told the artist.

"I put a protective coating on it and the owners will take their shoes off if they walk on it at all. They understand the value of the work, so they'll take care of it," he said.

By mid-morning, we were beginning to get hungry, so we went to the market, found some food stalls, and indulged ourselves with some exotic food from the east. I truly enjoyed getting to know Yeshua's world. It was in some ways bigger than mine. He moved more easily and frequently among people of different cultures, where I lived my life between the Temple in Jerusalem and my home in Bethany.

I was beginning to understand why Yeshua was so open to other people. He told me at one point, as we ate our meal, that God loves all people who have goodness in their hearts. Yeshua pointed to a young Greek boy helping an old blind Jewish man get his vegetables and then take him by the hand to lead him home. Yeshua said the boy was not the old man's relative.

"How do you know that?" I asked him.

"He lives next door to him. I saw them on days when I worked near here. I asked the boy one time if the man was his grandfather. He said no, that he just wanted to help the poor fellow. God loves a generous heart," Yeshua said.

I smiled, "Is this where your parable got its start?"

"Yes, I suppose maybe it did."

***

Later in the afternoon, we walked down the hillside and sat under the cool shade of a stand of trees, a gentle breeze keeping the flies away. Yeshua seemed melancholy as we gazed out on the valley below.

"There will come a time when I will leave this place, indeed I won't even be welcomed in my hometown," he said.

"Why is that?" I asked.

"Others will accept my words and the work I do, but the people of Nazareth will not."

"Yeshua, you aren't going to speak in the manner my father forbade you to speak, are you?"

"I was thirteen. I did not fully comprehend my own existence at that time. I still do not fully grasp it. However, I must follow the path that has been set before me. I will speak of many things that I have heard in the silence of my heart. The words are not my own but come from the One who sent me."

My face burned, and I felt tense.

"I don't expect you to understand Lazarus; I do pray that someday you will."

E. Ann McIntyre

Yeshua was a mystery to me. The way he spoke was unsettling. My father had let him off the hook, so to speak, when we younger. Now, however, I felt fear in my heart for him. *If indeed, he speaks as he did back then, Caiaphas will not be as lenient as was my father*.

***

I woke the next morning to a mystery: my priestly garments were gone, replaced by a set of well-made but plain robes. I knew the culprit was sitting outside my room on the roof.

"Yeshua?"

"Good morning Lazarus."

"Where are my clothes?"

"Hanging on the peg"

"No, they aren't my clothes. Perhaps they are yours?"

"No they are yours, my mother made them for you."

"That was nice of her. But where are the priestly robes Martha made for me?"

"In the wash bucket."

"How did they get in the wash bucket?"

"I put them in the wash bucket. Don't worry, my mother will have them all done up nicely for you when you head back in a couple of days."

I stuck my head out the curtain door. "So I have to wear these simple unadorned clothes for the duration of my stay in Galilee do I?"

"Seems so."

"I'll get you for this."

Yeshua laughed, "Want to pray?"

"As soon as I get dressed."

"I'll be right here waiting."
I wanted to wipe that smirk off his face.

E. Ann McIntyre

Chapter 14 The Fishermen

Capernaum was a good day's journey from Nazareth. We carried lunches Myriam had packed for us. It was a beautiful morning as we walked along the road and chatted about Yeshua's fishermen cousins. He explained that they worked all night bringing their catch to shore in the morning, which was one of the reasons he did not see them regularly; they worked at night, he during the day.

Yeshua said, "We should get to Capernaum just as they are about to set sail. Zebedee doesn't go out very often now. He leaves the hard work of catching the fish up to James and his partner, Simon bar Jonah. John is growing up fast; I think this is his first year out on the water with James."

"Do you think they will let us go out with them?" I asked.

"Can you swim?"

"I've never tried. So I suppose the answer is no."

"I can't yet, but I can float. James has this idea that if you can't swim you shouldn't get in a working fishing boat, but I have managed to weasel my way on board," Yeshua said with a smile.

By noon, we could see the grand Lake Gennesaret, or Sea of Galilee, in the distance. We passed through the town of Cana where we picked up some fruit to have with our lunch and enjoyed a refreshing drink of water at the well. The sun was high in the sky when we found a spot to have lunch in the shade of trees surrounded by a field full of flowers at the height of their summer bloom. "I don't think I have ever seen such a large number of flowers in one place before," I said.

"You know Lazarus, you worry too much about what you are to wear, what you are to put on. Just look at all these flowers as far as you can see, they neither spin nor toil, yet even Solomon in all his finest robes could not compare with the beauty God has given these grasses of the fields. For God this is beauty, simple beauty," Yeshua said.

"I think I'm getting your point. But I still want my robes back."

"You'll get them back."

***

The road to the lake took us past several towns, including Magdala where we stopped for more water. The hot sun was stirring up our thirst so we took advantage of every town well we came across.

It was late afternoon when we arrived at the lakeshore. Yeshua decided that rather than walk the remaining distance around the lake to Capernaum, we could hire a boat to sail us there. My sore legs and feet agreed. I had never walked so far in one day in my life. Yeshua seemed oblivious to the distance.

The boat master we found charged us a couple of denarii to take us to our destination. The lake was calm, so the sails did not have much wind to catch. Our boat master had to push with a long oar to get the boat out into deeper water so the sails could take over.

"Fishermen don't like calm waters," Yeshua said.

E. Ann McIntyre

"Why?" I asked as I looked over the bow. I could see clear to the bottom.

"The fish can see the nets coming and they dive deeper," he replied.

"Smart fish," I said.

"So there is a possibility James won't go out tonight."

"It's been like this for a couple of days. The fishing boats have to go way out to the middle of the lake to catch anything," the boat master said.

The trip to Capernaum was shorter than I expected as the town came quickly into view. It looked very nice from our vantage point on the lake. As we got closer to shore, the boat master had to start pushing with the oar again. As we landed, Yeshua pointed out the Zebedee boats moored a few yards away. I could see men milling around them.

Yeshua chose to walk in the water to greet his cousins. I followed behind him trying to keep my robes dry above the water. I was not successful in that endeavour.

"Hey, Sons of Zebedee have you caught anything today?" Yeshua yelled.

"Yeshua!" young John called out. He ran in our direction and threw his arms around Yeshua.

"Shalom, my young friend how are you doing? Do you remember my friend Lazarus?"

"Yes, I remember him from the Temple right?" John said as he walked arm-in-arm with Yeshua.

"That's correct young man," I said as I gave him a pat on the head.

James, his partner Simon and another young fellow waited for us on the boat and waved as we approached.

"Well this is a surprise. Nice to see you Lazarus. What are you doing in Galilee?" James said in greeting.

"Visiting Yeshua."

"Oh yes, Shalom cousin," James said with a laugh.

"Lazarus, this is my partner Simon bar Jonah and his brother Andrew," James said.

"Nice to meet you," I replied.

"Want to come up?" Simon reached his hand down to pull me aboard. I wasn't so sure he could. I was mistaken. Simon was a big strong fisherman and pulled me into the boat with one yank. I guess my weight was nothing compared to a fishing net full of fish.

"Are you going out tonight?" Yeshua asked.

"We aren't sure yet. We went out last night and only caught half a net all night." James said. "The tax collector Levi took most of the money we earned. In weather like this, it's hardly worth the effort."

"What kind of weather do you need?" I asked.

"A good constant stiff breeze will help. It stirs the water up and keeps the fish close to the surface. They like cool water. They don't like the water when it gets warm near the top so they'll go deeper into the lake for the cool water below. It makes them harder to catch," Simon explained.

"So do you know how to swim Lazarus? You know, just in case we do go out," James said.

"No, but I can learn. It can't be that hard."

"Oh we'll see now won't we?" James said slapping me on the back. Everyone laughed.

"You too Yeshua."

E. Ann McIntyre

Yeshua and I stood in our loincloths up to our knees in the water.

"Go out a little further," James said. We went up to our waist. "Okay, dive!"

I stretched out my arms and drove head-on into the water. I sank. I quickly put my feet on the bottom and tried to stand. I was up to my neck.

"What are you trying to do, James, drown me?" I said coughing up the water I managed to swallow. I turned around to face in the direction the laughter was coming from only to see that Yeshua was still standing there. He hadn't taken the dive.

"Come here City Boy, I'll teach you to swim," Simon said.

I stood in front of Simon who stretched out his arms under the water. "Lay on my arms," he said.

"Huh?"

"Lay on your stomach flat across my arms. I'll hold you until you have your arms and legs moving."

I did as Simon said. He held me. *Glory is he strong*. I thought.

"Move your arms and hands fast in a circular motion in front of you and kick with your feet," Simon ordered me. I did. He let go. I swam a few feet. I did not sink. I swam! I could hear the cheers. I tried to stand and acknowledge my triumph but I was out over my head. I sank.

The next thing I knew Simon grabbed me and pulled me up. I coughed up more water. "I guess I better teach you the dog paddle," he said.

"Well, you did swim, so I guess you can come out with us. But do try and master the dog paddle," James said.

"What's the dog paddle?" I asked.

"Ever watch a dog swim?" Simon asked me.

"No."

While Simon showed me how to swim like a dog, panting included, James was testing Yeshua's swimming skills. Instead of swimming as I did, he laid face down on the water, arms extended and floated like a dead man. James was not impressed.

"If the boat sank, how would you get to shore by just floating on the spot in the water?" James asked him.

Yeshua rolled over on his back, still floating, and said, "I'd walk."

***

As the sun was setting, a sudden offshore wind came up. "What perfect timing," James said. "Man your stations, everyone, we are going fishing!"

"What station do I have?" I asked.

"Get in front of the bow and push!" James said.

Yeshua and I did just that. Simon, James, John, and Andrew were on the boat pushing with oars. The boat floated free. Yeshua pulled himself on to the boat and left me standing in the water as the boat moved out fast.

"Well, Lazarus get in the boat!" James shouted.

"How? It's out too far for me to climb on."

"Swim."

I dove into the water and moved my arms and legs as hard and fast as I could. I made it to the side of the boat. Simon obligingly pulled me in. "Taught you well didn't I," he said with proud smile.

***

E. Ann McIntyre

Laying back in the bow of a boat looking at the stars from the middle of a big lake is an amazing experience. The fishing wasn't great, so they didn't need much help from me. I just sat back and watched. Yeshua did too. I don't think James was impressed. He kept giving us sidelong looks.

They were throwing their net over the same side of the boat, hauling in very few fish. At one point Yeshua suggested they trying casting their nets on the other side of the boat.

"So the carpenter from Nazareth is telling us how to catch fish is he?" James said with a weary smile.

John and Andrew picked up their net, a smaller one than the two James and Simon were using, and flung it over the side Yeshua had suggested. The young fellows' net was suddenly full of fish. It was much too heavy for the two to pull in by themselves. James and Simon jumped in to help pull the laden net into the boat. I looked at Yeshua and wondered *how did he know where the fish were?*

Simon had the answer, "That was a good guess Yeshua."

Yeshua looked at the water as some fish practically jumped into the boat. He looked at me and then looked at the water again and more fish jumped in the boat. If Yeshua was trying to convince me that he was responsible for the sudden catch, I wasn't buying it. However, he did have at least one believer. Ten-year-old John bar Zebedee stood looking at Yeshua, wide-eyed.

Chapter 15 Secrets

Unusually cold damp fall weather exasperated my father's aches and pains. Some days his legs hurt so much he could not get out of bed. The physician who attended him could not provide much relief. He told us to keep my father warm. Martha did her best. One night Abba started shivering uncontrollably. We tried covering him with warm blankets, but that did not help much. I told my sisters to go to bed, that I would stay with Abba until morning. They reluctantly agreed.

I sat beside my father's cot with the lamp burning low. Sometimes I would pray aloud or just quietly to myself. At one point, I felt his hand touch mine, and I realized he was awake.

"Are we alone my son?"

"Yes, Martha and Miriam have gone to bed. I told them I would stay with you."

"That is good. I need to talk to you," my father said as he drew in a deep breath and then coughed.

"Yes, Abba?"

"I have put my Will in safe keeping with the Scribes at the Temple. In it, I have left the house and guesthouse to Martha; I am sure you understand why. She has no husband to take care of her, and she has taken care of us and our home since your mother died. I thought it was only right."

I nodded. I couldn't speak. My throat was full.

"I left the vineyard to you and Miriam. I know how you love to work with it and perhaps you can encourage your sister to take a greater interest in it instead of whatever she has gotten herself into at the market in Jerusalem. It troubles me."

"Abba? What do you mean? I asked, "I didn't know that Miriam was working at the Jerusalem market."

"I don't know son. I didn't want to worry Martha, so I thought I would tell you. Perhaps you can, with some discretion, find out exactly what kind of work she is involved in."

I was concerned. I assured my father I would find out what Miriam was doing.

My father laid there quietly for a few moments. Again, he reached out for my hand. His breathing was laboured. He seemed emotional.

"Lazarus, do you remember what Yosef of Nazareth said about my father having been the one who performed the dedication ceremony for Yeshua after his birth in Bethlehem?"

"Yes, Abba. I remember."

"What I'm about to tell you, you must keep to yourself. It is something I haven't been able to get out of my mind since Yosef told us that story," he coughed again. I held a cloth to his mouth.

"Before my father Simeon died, God fulfilled a promise he made to him in a dream. God promised him that he would live to see the Messiah," Abba's breathing grew even more laboured as he spoke with much emotion.

"My father told me that a young woman and a slightly older man brought their baby boy to the temple to be circumcised. They had come from Bethlehem where the baby was born. My father was praying the prayers of dedication when he experienced a revelation from the Most High. He went out to greet the family and looked at the baby. It was then that he knew he was looking at the Messiah, the future glory of Israel. He had a vision of a sword piercing the mother's heart. An old woman at the Temple by the name of Anna experienced the same vision." My father almost lost his breath completely. I put my hand under his head to lift it hoping it would help him breathe.

"He told me that he prayed his children and his children's children might come to know the Messiah. He said that the Most High assured him that his descendants would indeed know this truth for themselves."

I started to choke, "Abba, did your father tell you the names of the baby's parents?"

He shook his head, "He only knew the baby's name. His name was…"

I waited for my father to continue, to tell me the baby's name but my father could no longer speak. He had breathed his last breath.

I laid my face in the palm of his open hand and wept.

***

Many mourners came to Bethany to grieve with us. The current Sanhedrin members and former members were there, as were officials from the Roman court, which surprised me. They told me that they had great respect for my father and hoped to continue that relationship with me. It took me a while to realize they were talking about our wine.

E. Ann McIntyre

The most difficult time after a death in a family is when everybody leaves and the family faces the vacuum left by the dearly departed. Caiaphas told me to take a week off to tidy up my father's affairs and rest. I was surprised at his generosity and concern. He added that he had something to discuss with me when I returned to the Temple the following week.

There really wasn't much "tidying up" to do. Father had transferred all his business dealings to me over the last year. Father had also left his legal affairs in good order so the transfer of property was very smooth. Martha was a property owner, which was a rare status for a woman to have. Father had done the right thing; she truly deserved to be a woman of status.

My main concern was what my father had revealed to me about my sister Miriam, just before he died. I needed to find out what she was doing in Jerusalem. When I asked her a few days after our father's funeral, she just shrugged and said she was working in a stall at the market. She wouldn't tell me what she was selling. I had a promise to keep to Abba; I would find out what she was doing.

***

I hated the very idea that I was spying on my sister, but Miriam's silence on the nature of her work in Jerusalem forced me to act. A couple of weeks after our father's death I decided to follow her. I usually left for the Temple early in the morning so I never knew when Miriam left for Jerusalem. Mid-week I decided to wait in the vineyard for Miriam to leave the house. I waited a long time for her to exit; when she finally did, it was late afternoon. I followed at a discrete distance.

She had her face well covered so it would be hard for anyone to identify her. She made the turn to the market just past the Zebedee house. Miriam did not stop at any market stall. She kept going. She never looked back.

I continued to follow her until she turned down an alley. I stopped, afraid that she would see me; I leaned against the corner of the last building. I saw Miriam open a door halfway down the alley and go in. I stepped back and man came up to me and said, "Well, are you going to her or not?"

"What?" I said.

"That woman you were following, are you going to her? If you aren't I certainly will."

"I... I... don't know what you are a talking about," I said trying to comprehend what was going on here.

"That woman is a harlot. Don't you know that? Are you dense?" he said.

I couldn't breathe. I was shocked. He shook his head, walked around me and went to my sister's door. I watch in horror as Miriam let him in. I raged. I ran down the alley and hammered my fist on the door. "Miriam, Miriam," I shouted.

The man, half dressed, opened it. "What do you want?" he yelled.

"I am getting my sister," I pushed him aside, looked into the darken interior, and saw Miriam sitting on the edge of the bed naked. She screamed at me. "Get out of here Lazarus! You have no business being here." A struggle ensued. I tried to get her clothes on her. She fought back. Her customer left. Miriam continued to fight me.

"You can't do this, Miriam, please come home with me. Please!" I begged her.

"Get out, get out."

I didn't want to hurt her but the struggle was turning into a fight. She shocked me with a punch to my right eye. It hurt. I stepped back. She took the moment of my instability to push me completely out the door, slamming it shut behind me. I heard it lock.

I pounded the door with both hands and tried to push it open. I could hear Miriam sobbing. "Go away, Lazarus. I am not going home, not ever. I'm through being your nice, quiet sister," she screeched.

I backed away. I lost the fight. I lost my sister. Devastated, I turned towards home. I would have to face telling Martha what my father could not; our little sister was a harlot.

**

Martha was pained and grieved with the news of our sister's lifestyle. She held a cold compress to my eye to ease the swelling from Miriam firm punch.

Martha sobbed, "Oh, Lazarus, what are we to do? I feel awful. I had no idea that this was what she was doing. She told me she was selling women's clothing at the market. I had no reason not to believe her."

I did not tell her that Father had suspected something wasn't right, perhaps it was the hours of the day when she went to and from the house that triggered his suspicions. I would never know. For Martha and me it was a terrible blow. We had lost our father a few weeks prior to this and now we had lost our dear sister. We wondered whether she would ever come home again.

It never occurred to me that my pursuit of Miriam would start tongues wagging about the priest from the Temple being beaten up by his sister the harlot, but that is what happened. Apparently, Miriam's customer that night had a drink or two and started telling tales in the local public house. The story got back to Caiaphas, who sent for me.

***

I stood in the quarters of the High Priest facing Caiaphas with my black eye. I was nervous, to say the least.

"I have heard about your troubles with your sister. I hope you get that settled soon," he said.

"I tried, but it was in vain. I could not get her to come home," I said.

"Did she give you that black eye?"

"Yes, sir."

"I see. I suggest you get that issue resolved before I have to take action."

I swallowed hard. By "action," Caiaphas meant, "stoning."

"Besides," he continued, "It wouldn't look good for a member of the Sanhedrin to have a sister who is a whore, now would it?"

"No, sir. Sanhedrin?"

"Yes, that is actually why I called you here. You come from a long line of High Priests, and I think it is time you joined the Sanhedrin, Eleazar." Caiaphas said.

E. Ann McIntyre

"Yes, sir. Thank you. I will serve to the best of my ability and with honor," I replied.

"Good. The first meeting for you will be in two days in the Hall of the Sanhedrin. We look forward to welcoming you."

I bowed and made my exit.

Chapter 16 Storm Clouds

Yosef Caiaphas sat on the President's chair surrounded by the seventy members of the Sanhedrin. I was the newest member. I stood as he welcomed me to the highest court of Jewish law. Those who knew why I had a black eye, and those who wondered how I got the black eye, were staring at me. Fortunately, Caiaphas made no mention of my personal issues. I sat down and Caiaphas formally opened the meeting.

"I have received notice from Tiberius Caesar that he is appointing a new Prefect for the Provinces of Judea and Samaria. His name is Pontius Pilate. He will replace Valerius Gratus in coming months. The Emperor has provided little information about the new Prefect. He says here that Pilate has distinguished himself in the battlefields of the empire.

"As usual we should remain cautious in our dealings with Roman authorities so as not to provide any justification for their intrusion into our day-to-day lives. Our obligations to the Prefect are to keep the peace and to ensure the people within our jurisdiction do so as well."

Uncomfortable silence greeted Caiaphas' words. As it is said, "Better the devil you know." I heard someone whisper behind me, "Military types never stop fighting wars." The Sanhedrin as a body was concerned as to why Tiberius had made this particular appointment.

E. Ann McIntyre

***

I had made it to the Sanhedrin, an expected step in my life as a priest, but I was unsettled. That evening at supper, Martha asked me what it was like sitting in the auspicious chamber of the Sanhedrin. We tried to keep our conversation upbeat, but it was difficult, we both had only one thing on our minds. We were worried about what might happen to our sister.

I went up to the roof to pray. I should have felt happy about being on the great council, but my heart was weighed down. I prayed to God for my sister. I prayed that He would bring her home to us, something I could not do on my own. I went back downstairs to my room and slept with a heavy heart.

They dragged Miriam through the streets and brought her before the Sanhedrin council. I could not defend her against their accusations. They declared her guilty and sentenced her to death by stoning.

Because Miriam had brought shame to our family, Caiaphas ordered me to cast the first stone. I could feel the stone in my hand; I turned it over and over as I tightened my fist around it. I stared at my sister as she sat on the ground surrounded by men holding stones in their hands, waiting for me to throw the first one at her.

Her eyes pleaded with me, the tears rolled down her face. My hands were shaking. The voices around me shouted, "Throw, throw the stone and kill the harlot." I lifted my arm to cast the stone but something or someone stopped the forward motion of my hand. I heard a voice, "Let the one who is without fault cast the first stone." I turned to look at whoever said those words, I saw no one.

Lazarus of Bethany

I woke from the dream in a lather and shaking. "Miriam, where are you? Please come home," I prayed. I got up from my cot still shaken by the terrible nightmare. I put my cloak around me, grabbed a lantern, and headed to the roof. I sat outside my old room and tried to pray. My heart was racing, my mind too full of thoughts of my sister for the prayers to come. I missed her so much. Martha and I were not a family without Miriam. I didn't care what the Law said. I wanted my sister back. I could never cast a stone at her. I laid down on the roof, arm over my eyes and wept.

Oh, dear sweet Miriam where are you? Why did you take this path? Is it my fault? Were we as a family so busy attending to my future that we ignored you? Exhausted, I drifted off.

***

I felt a shake, "Lazarus, Lazarus, wake up."

I rolled over on my back and looked up into the eyes of my older sister.

"What are you doing up here? I searched all over the house and vineyard but I couldn't find you. Your robes were there, so I knew you hadn't gone to the Temple," she said.

"I had a bad dream last night. It was about Miriam. We need to find her, Martha."

"I haven't stopped looking for her, Lazarus. I go to town daily, but I've never been able to locate her. Nobody seems to even know her name." Martha looked downcast.

E. Ann McIntyre

I sat up on my elbows. "You don't suppose she has changed her name, do you? So that we couldn't find her?"

"That's possible, but changed it to what?

"Can you think of any name she might have used in play as a child?" I said.

"Not off hand," Martha said shaking her head.

There was silence between us as we both tried to think of a way to locate our wayward sister.

***

There was no peace in my life, not at home and not at the Temple. The new Roman Prefect had taken up his residence in the Governor's palace in Caesarea, but it seemed he didn't know a thing about governing Judea. Only coming to Jerusalem during feast celebrations, Pontius Pilate had barely set foot in Jerusalem when he provoked the anger and rage of our people and the entire Sanhedrin, myself included.

It was early in the morning the day after the Sabbath when there was a frantic knock on our door. A Temple attendant handed me an urgent message from the Sanhedrin. I was called to a meeting at the Temple, within the hour. I quickly dressed in my formal robes and headed to the city.

I was halfway down the road from Bethany when I heard the roar of the crowds. People were running past me to see what was going on. It wasn't until I stepped through the Temple gate that I saw what can only be described as a total desecration of our holy place. Hanging from the ramparts and walls of the Temple was the Emperor's golden image emblazoned on standards. I was horrified.

I hurried to the Hall of the Sanhedrin; the noise was deafening. Yosef Caiaphas tried in vain to gain control of the meeting. Members demanded the immediate removal of the standards.

"Please, please, sit down; we must act as one if we are to be successful at getting those standards removed," Caiaphas said.

The members finally sat and listened to the President of the gathered council. Caiaphas called for three members to join him in a meeting with the Prefect. He asked for our oldest member, my former master, the Pharisee Yosef of Arimathea, Simon the Sadducee, and a priest – me, the newest member. We needed to organize our presentation to Pilate, hoping he would see the error of his ways and take down the standards. I was nervous. I had never before been involved in such an important action on behalf of our people.

Caiaphas had arranged for an afternoon meeting at the governor's palace, a place I was familiar with because of our wine sales there. I knew Governor Gratus, but I had yet to meet his successor, Pontius Pilate.

We gathered in the chambers of the High Priest to hammer out our presentation. We would present arguments based on our history and traditions. We had no way of knowing if Pilate had any knowledge of our traditions. We were about to find out.

Early afternoon saw the four of us walking over to the palace for our meeting with Pilate. The demeanour of the man should have triggered our retreat; but Caiaphas was determined to effect a change in the situation with the standards, now.

E. Ann McIntyre

We were each supposed to give a presentation, but that did not happen. Pilate would only let Caiaphas speak. Pilate feigned he was listening. In the end, he said the standards would remain where they were and kicked us out of the palace.

Caiaphas was enraged and began to write what would become a series of letters to Tiberius. The letter campaign worked and the standards eventually came down, months after they went up.

It was not the last of Pilate's incursions into our affairs. The High Priest, indeed the Sanhedrin was responsible for the financial health of the Temple. Pilate took it upon himself to take our money out of the Treasury to finance Roman aqueduct projects. More letters to Tiberius followed. There was no telling what this man would do. We were relieved when the festivals were over, and he retreated to Caesarea. That, it seems, was a false sense of relief.

Pilate's activities stirred the interest and concern of the Zealots in the area. They began a series of attacks on Roman soldiers and officials, led by a man named Barabbas. Those attacks not only got the attention of Pilate but also Caiaphas. He knew there would be retaliation from Pilate. Pilate had called Caiaphas to his office to warn him. The political tensions in the area were growing. No one knew when or how the hammer would come down.

Chapter 17 A Voice, A Mad Man, and a Coward

Caiaphas learned there was a man, possibly an Essene, preaching and baptizing on the banks of the Jordan River. I was one of the seven council members from the Sanhedrin sent on a mission to find him. Caiaphas armed us with questions and demands; we were to bring back answers. People baptized by this man came to the Temple and spread the news that the baptizer was the Messiah. Remembering what my father said before he died, I wanted to find out first-hand if indeed the Messiah had come.

The seven of us trudged along the old dirt road to the Jordan River; finding a caravan to take us there was nearly impossible. Determined to track down the Zealots who were attacking his soldiers on the roadways, Pilate had ordered a ban on caravan travel throughout Judea.

We met people coming from the Jordan excitedly discussing the baptizer. We found out his name was John bar Zachariah, and he was at the river near the town of Bethany-on-the Jordon, (not to be confused with my hometown). We trudged on.

There were about fifty people milling around on both banks of the river. I could not pick anyone out as a person of interest in terms of our mission. Master Nicodemus pointed to a group of men sitting in a sheltered area across the river and downstream from us. One was wearing what looked like animal skins.

E. Ann McIntyre

He looked in our direction, stood up, grabbed a large staff, and ventured out into the river. He placed both his hands on his staff and glared at us.

Simon the Sadducee stepped forward and called to the man, "Who are you? Are you the Messiah or are we to look for another?'

"I am not the Messiah."

"Who are you then, are you the Prophet?"

"I am not."

"Tell us who you are then. We must take an answer back to those who sent us. What do you say of yourself?"

"I am *the voice crying in the wilderness, preparing the way of the Lord.*"

"If you are not the Messiah or the Prophet, why do you baptize?'

"I baptize with water, but there is one coming after me, he is among you, whose sandals I am not fit to untie! He will baptize with the Holy Spirit and fire!"

It seemed like the man himself was breathing fire as his voice reverberated off the river. We were riveted. I thought to myself, *He says he is not the Messiah. He says there is someone out there who is coming after him. Who would that be*?

I eyed the people who had gathered around this man, he obviously had a number of disciples. The two young men who had been sitting with the baptizer stepped out of the shadows. I recognized them. One was John bar Zebedee, the other was Andrew, the brother of Simon the fisherman.

We had enough information to take to Caiaphas. We turned to go back to Jerusalem; Master Yosef of Arimathea touched my arm.

"My eyes are failing me. I see someone standing with the baptizer; do you recognize who it is, Lazarus?"

"John bar Zebedee and Andrew bar Jonah are there with him," I said without looking back.

"No, it is someone else."

I looked back over my shoulder. I was surprised. "That's my friend Yeshua bar Yosef from Nazareth. I wonder what he is doing here." I called out to him. I waved. He did not respond.

"Apparently he is getting baptized," Master Yosef said.

At that very moment, John the Baptizer plunged Yeshua into the water. When he came up from the water, there was a sound of thunder from a cloudless sky. Yosef, Nicodemus, and I looked at each other.

"What was that?" I said.

"A thunderous voice," Yosef responded.

"I heard it too," said Nicodemus.

"I didn't hear a voice, I heard thunder. Where did it come from? What did the voice say?"

"I think I heard the words *This is my son*," Master Nicodemus said.

"I'm confused. Whose son? Who said it?" I asked.

"I don't know. I didn't hear it clearly." Master Yosef rubbed his white beard. "You are going to have to help me again, Lazarus. What is that flying around Yeshua?"

"Looks like a dove."

We watched as Yeshua turned and went up the embankment. The baptizer waved to John and Andrew as if to tell them to go with Yeshua. I continued to watch until the three men disappeared from sight.

"Yeshua is probably going to go back to Galilee with the young men," I said.

"Hmm, I don't know Lazarus, there's something going on here. I feel it," Master Yosef said. Master Nicodemus nodded in agreement. Other than thunder from a clear blue sky, I did not see or hear anything unusual.

We talked among ourselves on the way back to Jerusalem, and we decided that this baptizer did not pose any threat or concern to the established order of our way of life. We were concerned about someone he said was coming after him. Master Yosef did not say a word. He just kept looking back and rubbing his beard.

***

Pontius Pilate continued to incur the anger of our people, and protest mounted against his use of the Temple's treasury for his projects. Caiaphas tried to calm the crowd. One day Pilate decided that he himself would address the people.

Pilate chose to speak to the crowd from the Praetorium. I was standing with other members of the Sanhedrin near the Governor's palace on the edge of the square. It was just before noon when Pilate stepped out to speak.

I noticed that in spite of the large crowd there was a conspicuous lack of soldiers. My guess was that Pilate was hoping for a conciliatory meeting, which would be unusual for him. Pilate spoke for a few minutes on how the aqueducts would benefit all citizens of Jerusalem, bringing much needed fresh water to the city. Some people yelled at him, "Not with our sacred Temple money!"

Pilate just shook his head as the crowd grew more hostile. Finally, he threw his arms up in disgust. That gesture was a signal. Roman soldiers were indeed present in the square, camouflaged in ordinary street robes. At Pilate's signal, they threw off their disguises and began a murderous rampage through the crowd.

Pushed up against a wall with a screaming crowd pressing against me, I struggled to get away. The soldiers were moving in on us, slashing with their swords as they came. I saw an opening to the street and made a dash for it. I ran and did not look back. I could hear the horrifying screams behind me.

I ran out the Beautiful Gate towards Bethany with the stampede of panic-stricken people. Running uphill through the Garden of Olives took the wind out of me, so I had to stop and catch my breath. I looked across the road and saw a man haemorrhaging from his leg. He was breathing hard and shaking. He reached out to me and cried, "Help me, priest!"

I hesitated; I backed away from him and continued up the road. Then, like a bolt of lightning; Yeshua's parable came back to me; suddenly I was the priest walking away from the injured man. I stopped and looked back; someone else, who gave me a brief glance, was treating the man. It was a Samaritan helping the stricken Jew.

Shaken, I felt sick to my stomach. I was ashamed. *How did he know? He couldn't possibly have seen this day,* I thought. I turned my eyes away from the two men and continued towards home. I met Martha coming from Bethany.

E. Ann McIntyre

"I heard what happened. I came to see if you were well," she said.

"I'm fine but there are many who have been killed or injured."

"I see a man who needs help," Martha said. She ran down the road to the man I had passed by, and the Samaritan who was assisting him. I watched as Martha helped to bind the man's wound. "Can you help, Lazarus? If we can get him to our house I can dress his wound properly."

I went back down the road and did as Martha asked; the Samaritan and I locked our hands under his legs so we could carry him. Martha supported him from behind. We walked slowly up the hill to our home. We laid the man down on the cushions in our living area. Martha made strips from a clean cloth and bandaged the man's wound.

"What is your name?" Martha asked the injured man.

"Philip," he replied, "Thank you all for helping me. I thought I was going to die on the road."

I stood in embarrassed silence next to the Samaritan. Finally, I whispered to him, "You are more righteous in the sight of God than I." That was the point of Yeshua's parable; I just proved him right.

"He is in good hands now. I will depart, Shalom," the Samaritan said. He bowed to Martha, Philip, and me.

"What was that about?" Martha asked.

I didn't answer because I didn't know what to say. Martha looked at me. She pursed her mouth and shook her head. She knew what I had done.

Chapter 18 Disciples

Philip went in and out of consciousness over the following few days. In spite of Martha's best efforts to bring healing to his wound, it festered. Martha sent me to find a physician to help her save Philip, as she feared he might die.

I managed to locate a Greek physician by the name of Lucanus who was new to the area. He was young, about eighteen, and acknowledged he did not have much experience yet, but with so many people in Jerusalem injured, physicians were in high demand. This young man would have to do.

Lucanus said that he had already treated a number of injured persons from the terrible attack on ordinary citizens. He would do his best to save Philip. When we got to the house, Lucanus examined Martha's patient. He was impressed with how well Martha had cared for the wound. He said that Philip was suffering from an infection caused by the soldier's weapon. During the physician's examination, Philip began to speak incoherently.

"Rabboni, Rabboni, I need you, please help me," he cried out.

"Who is your teacher?" Lucanus asked him.

Philip's eyes opened, but he could barely focus; he slurred the words, "Yeshua of Nazareth."

Martha and I looked at each other; our friend was his Master. We also knew that Yeshua had healed our father; perhaps that was why Philip was calling for him.

"Philip, where is Yeshua now? Do you know?" I asked him.

Philip had a hard time getting his words out; however, I heard, "Jerusalem in a week, before Passover," Philip passed out again.

"Do you know this Yeshua of Nazareth?" Lucanus asked.

"Yes, he is our friend, and we know he is a healer," I responded.

"There is not much I can do for this man's infection except wait and hope he can fight it off. Although I am sceptical about healers, I'm always open to learning from real healers in different cultures," Lucanus said.

"Do you think Philip can survive for a week?" Martha asked.

Lucanus shook his head. "I don't know."

"Lazarus, do you think you can find Yeshua? Maybe he'll come to help Philip," Martha said.

As I was about to answer a shadow darkened the doorway. "Shalom, my friends."

It was Yeshua. He touched my shoulder, greeted Martha and Physician Lucanus. Yeshua knelt beside Philip. He ran his hand down Philip's leg and asked Martha and I to leave he and Lucanus alone with Philip.

We stepped out into our courtyard and found several people waiting for Yeshua. I recognized a few of them: James and John bar Zebedee, Simon bar Jonah, and his brother Andrew.

"Shalom, why are you all here?" I asked them.

"We are disciples of Yeshua now." James said, "And he came to help Philip."

"How did he know about Philip?"

"He just knew to come to him. Yeshua is a great teacher, Lazarus. He is also a healer." Simon said.

"I knew about his gift of healing. What is he teaching?" I asked them.

"About the Kingdom of God. Have you ever heard him teach?" James said.

"No, we haven't."

"Well you must come to the Temple later he said he would go there to teach today."

James then introduced the rest of Yeshua's disciples gathered in our courtyard. There was Matthew a former tax collector, another James, Judas bar Iscariot, Jude, and another Simon. There was one young woman accompanying them, her name was Mariam from Magdala. There were more of the group waiting on the street. It seemed to me that Yeshua had quite the following.

Just as James finished his round of introductions, Philip appeared in the doorway. Martha ran up to him and said, "Are you well?"

"Yes, I am fine, thanks to Yeshua," Philip replied.

Yeshua and Lucanus followed Philip out the door. All the disciples ran forward and embraced Philip.

Well, he did it again. I thought. I glanced at Lucanus, who shook his head with a look of amazement on his face. Yeshua had the physician convinced.

Martha invited everyone to stay and have lunch. "There's plenty." It seemed Martha's kettle of soup was bottomless. Even she was amazed. I think everyone had seconds. Mariam of Magdala leaned forward and told Martha that food never ran out when Yeshua was around. The two women laughed. I felt suddenly lonesome for my sister Miriam. She would love this gathering.

I cornered James in our sitting room. I wanted to find out why he and the other fishermen had become Yeshua's disciples.

"Do you remember when you and Yeshua came out fishing with us, and Yeshua suggested we throw our nets off the other side of the boat?"

"Yes, and John and Andrew did and caught more than a net full."

"That's right. Simon and I laughed it off as a coincidence," James said, with a pause in his voice. "Well, it happened again. This time we had been out fishing all night, and we hadn't caught a single fish."

"John and Andrew had been disciples of John the Baptizer when he baptized Yeshua and told them to follow Yeshua instead."

"I was there when that happened; I saw them go with him. I didn't hear what was said."

"They spent some time with him and brought him to us."

"So, why is that so special? He is your cousin," I reasoned.

"Well yes you are right but it's what they told us. They said that the Baptizer had told them he was the expected one."

"Oh, really? And you believed them just like that."

"No, we didn't, at least not right away. We were laughing at them when Yeshua told us to go back out and throw our nets in the lake again. We weren't going to go at first, but John and Andrew jumped into the boat and said "what do you have to lose except sleep" so, we went back out."

"We did as Yeshua said and threw our nets back in the water."

"Don't tell me - they were suddenly full of fish," I interjected.

"Our nets were so full of fish we couldn't lift them into the boat," James recalled. "We had to bring the boat in with the nets still in the water."

"Once we got to shore I ran to get my father, he was incredulous. It was then that Yeshua invited us to be his disciples. He said he would make us *Fishers of men*" and we would see greater things from him. We've been with him ever since."

"I'm willing to bet Zebedee isn't thrilled about that," I said.

James laughed, "No, he isn't, he has hired men doing the work now. He was annoyed with Yeshua. He told him to get his own sons. Mother, however, is thrilled. She hopes Yeshua will make John and I his right and left-hand men when he takes the throne of David."

"You don't mind if I reserve judgement on that score, do you? I mean has he declared himself to be the Messiah or are you, folks, just bantering that around?"

"No, he hasn't directly said so," James admitted.

"I would suggest you leave it like that. If Caiaphas gets wind of those "Messiah" rumours it would spell big trouble for Yeshua," I said.

I continued to listen to the lively stories about Yeshua's many healings and his teachings. There were so many conversations going on at the same time I could only listen to snippets of the stories, Yeshua,

E. Ann McIntyre

who sat there with a grin on his face, watched me the whole time. He wanted me to hear all this. He had become what he always wanted to be, rabbi of the people. Intrigued by my friend's reported activities, I was also concerned at how his disciples were interpreting those activities.

Chapter 19 My Father's House, My Sister's Keeper

Yeshua and his disciples left for Jerusalem in the early afternoon. Martha and I stayed home to prepare for our expected guest. Martha had invited Mariam of Magdala to stay with us for the duration of Yeshua's visit to Jerusalem. Yeshua and his male disciples would stay at the Zebedee house.

Martha was planning for Mariam to stay in my room. "Why don't you just give her Miriam's room?" I queried. Martha gave me a forlorn look. "Lazarus, I haven't given up the hope that our sister will come home someday soon. I would prefer to have her room available for her when she does."

"I'm sorry Martha. I should have thought that over better, of course, we would keep it for her. I'll move to the roof."

"You can use the guesthouse if you want."

"I'm leaving that free for Yeshua if he wants to stay with us."

With our sleeping arrangements settled, I decided to go to the Temple and listen to Yeshua teach. I thought it was a good opportunity for me to hear his words of wisdom for myself.

***

I entered the Court of the Gentiles I found myself greeted by a stampede of sacrificial beasts. I attempted to corral them with little success. I thought they must have gotten loose from someone's pen, so I looked around to see who had lost them. That is when I saw the chaos further up the court. People were yelling things like "How dare you!" and "On whose authority do you do this?"

I could not see who was causing the disturbance, but I could hear the crashing of tables and chinking of money to the ground. I could see the priests and Pharisees looking down from the top level of the Temple at whoever was doing this.

Loud protests continued to emanate from the scene in front of me. I ran halfway up the stairs so I could get a better look at what was going on. I could see a hand brandishing a crude whip. Whoever he was, he was quickly turning over more tables and releasing more animals from their makeshift pens. Then he stopped and there was sudden silence. I ran further up the stairs. It was Yeshua.

"This Temple is a house of prayer, but you vipers have turned my Father's house into a den of thieves!"

He was angry, consumed with the task. His actions caught the attention of the Chief Priest Ananias who rapidly descended the stairs to confront him.

"Who do you think you are? You have no business disrupting the Passover preparations!"

More tables went crashing to the cement as Yeshua continued his rampage. I was aghast. This was unacceptable behaviour. I had to talk to him. I made chase.

"Eleazar bar Boethius, my chambers now!" It was Caiaphas. I stopped my pursuit of Yeshua and nervously climbed the remaining stairs to the chambers of the High Priest.

Caiaphas was facing the wall when I entered the room behind him. He cleared his throat.

"I understand you know that man."

"Yes, sir."

"Who is he?"

"Yeshua bar Yosef from Nazareth."

"A Galilean is he? Is he one of those Zealots responsible for the attacks on the Romans?" Caiaphas demanded to know.

"No sir, he is a carpenter by trade, but he has become a rabbi in recent months."

"That is not how a rabbi behaves in the Temple. From now on if he is going to be in the Temple he must have my permission to teach," he said sternly. "Furthermore, I suggest you find your friend and tell him that if there are any more outbursts like that I will have to deal with him as prescribed by the Law."

I stood there for a few moments not quite knowing what to do. Finally, Caiaphas said, "Go find this Yeshua of Nazareth, and tell him this is the only warning he will get from me."

***

Finding Yeshua was not easy. I hurried past the mess he had left behind in the Court of the Gentiles. The first place I checked was the Zebedee house. Neither he nor any of his disciples were there. I continued to check other areas around the Temple. Yeshua had made himself scarce fast.

I started to head back to the Temple when I heard a crowd of people shouting, "Harlot! Harlot!

Take the adulteress to him." I looked around the far outside corner of the temple and saw Yeshua sitting on the lower step. There was a woman crumpled on the ground in front of him. A number of men were standing around, some holding stones.

"Master, what do you say? We caught this woman in the act of adultery. What should be done with her?" they demanded.

I moved in a little closer and to my horror, the woman at the feet of Yeshua was my sister Miriam. I staggered back against the Temple wall.

Yeshua did not do or say anything right away. He sat down and ran his finger through the dirt on the step. Finally, he stood and glanced at my sister lying at his feet. Then he looked around at the men who encircled her, menacingly tossing the stones in their hands.

"Let the one who is without sin cast the first stone," Yeshua told them.

Yeshua sat back down and waited. One by one the men dropped their stones and walked away until not one of her accusers remained. "Woman, where are the ones who condemned you?" he said to her.

"There is no one," Miriam said.

"Then, neither do I condemn you. Go and sin no more."

Miriam slowly got up off the ground, dusted herself off and turned in my direction. She saw me. She lowered her eyes. Yeshua stood up, put his arm around Miriam's shoulders and led her to me. I slowly moved forward and embraced my sister. We both wept.

"May I come home, Lazarus?" Miriam said through her tears.

Lazarus of Bethany

"Oh my dear sister, yes, yes, please do. Martha has your room ready for you. She... we have been waiting for this day."

I looked over Miriam's head and whispered "Thank you" to Yeshua; his eyes were swimming with emotion. He loved my family as much as I did. I was grateful.

Still holding Miriam tightly I turned towards Bethany. I ignored the whistles and catcalls as we made our way through the streets of Jerusalem. I did not care what other people thought. My prayer was answered; I was bringing my sister home. *"Thank you, God,"* I prayed, *"thank you for Yeshua."*

Yeshua and Mariam of Magdala joined us on the walk home. It was a beautiful late afternoon. I was feeling joyful. I still had a message to deliver to my friend, but for now, it could wait. As we neared Bethany, I tried to imagine the look on Martha's face when she opened the door. I did not have to wait long. We entered our courtyard and I encouraged Miriam to go ahead of me. I bit my tongue trying to be quiet. Miriam gently knocked on the door and waited. It opened.

I will never forget the sight of my two sisters twirling about in a joyful dance, amid the dust and the squeals; it made me dizzy just watching them. Martha could hardly breathe as she tried to ask how this came about. I just pointed at Yeshua. I do not think Yeshua was quite ready for Martha's passionate *"thank you"*, and I am not sure Martha's display of gratitude was entirely appropriate. I was not about to play the role of law enforcer – at least not at that moment. Yeshua gave me a smile and an elbow as he walked by me.

E. Ann McIntyre

He was obviously pleased. I just rolled my eyes at him.

"Lazarus," Martha said when she finally found her voice, "you must go out to the winery and get your best wine. We must celebrate; our sister was lost and has been found again!"

Martha had been saving up her best cakes for this day. She put out quite the feast for our sister's return. Yeshua and Mariam of Magdala rejoiced with us well into the evening. It was during the meal that Mariam told us the she and John bar Zebedee were going to be married in Cana the week after Passover.

"I know that you and John know each other well, and I think it would be wonderful if the three of you could come to our wedding," she said.

"We would love to," I responded. "Would you like us to bring the wine?"

"Absolutely! That would be wonderful. Bring plenty!"

***

The roof had always been a sanctuary for Yeshua and me, that night was no different. It had been some time since the two of us were together to talk and pray. This time the prayer was grace-filled; the talk was a little more difficult than usual.

We stood facing Jerusalem and prayed the evening psalms. Yeshua quoted from the prophets that night, it was as though he knew what I had to talk to him about; he prayed. *"Zeal for your house consumes me."*

I felt as though I was in my father's place, it was my turn to admonish my friend. After what he had done for my family, it was a difficult task, so I began with a soft tone and a question. "Yeshua, why did you rip through the vendors at the Temple?"

"The Temple is not a marketplace; it is a sacred place of prayer."

"The animals for the Passover sacrifice have been sold there for years. You know that. They have to be sold nearby, and people need to be able to convert their foreign money."

"There are more things being sold there than just the animals," he said. "Goods being sold in the Temple belong in the main market in the city; not in the Temple. The moneychangers are cheating people on the rightful value for their money, making huge profits on the backs of poor people. The Temple administration should stop such cheating, but they don't because some of that profit ends up in their hands too."

His eyes flashed as they caught the dim light of the single lamp we had burning. He walked to the edge of the roof and leaned against the half wall looking in the direction of Jerusalem. "Go ahead Lazarus, tell me what you have to tell me."

He had his back to me, so I went and stood beside him. I leaned my left arm on the top of the half wall as I tried to look at him, but the darkness obscured his face. "Yeshua, I have to tell you that Caiaphas had some very strong words for what you did today. What I bring is a warning, the only warning you will ever get from him. Caiaphas said that if you ever do anything like that again he would bring the full force of the Law down on you. He also said you are not to teach in the Temple without his permission."

E. Ann McIntyre

Yeshua turned his head sharply in my direction. "I need his permission to teach in my Father's house?" I heard him chuckle. "I will speak when and where I choose."

"Yeshua, Caiaphas is a powerful man. After the slaughter of our people by the Romans this week, Caiaphas will not put up with any troublemakers. Yeshua, please, you have no idea what he is capable of."

"I know better than you realize Lazarus. The time for that confrontation will come, but not yet."

Chapter 20 Martha, Miriam and Me - Lessons

Passover celebrations were peaceful at the Temple; thankfully, there were no disruptions to the festival. Yeshua slipped in and out of the city without much notice. He dropped into our house for dinner before leaving for Galilee and the wedding of his two disciples in Cana.

Martha was busy in the kitchen preparing the meal, which was a woman's custom. Yeshua and I sat in the sitting room lounging back on the cushions. Yeshua was telling one of his stories, a parable about a woman losing a shekel, turning the whole house upside down until she found it, and then rejoicing with her friends. Miriam was sitting near Yeshua, soaking in his story, while I sipped my third goblet of wine, half-listening, half-sleeping, and drifting in and out of attentiveness. That did not last long.

Martha stormed into the sitting room and complained to Yeshua about Miriam's absence from the meal preparations. "Yeshua, don't you care that I am in the kitchen preparing the meal by myself while my sister sits here listening to you? Tell Miriam to get up and help me!"

I abruptly sat up and stared at Yeshua. *What's he going to do about this?*

"Martha, Martha," he said, "you are concerned with many things, but only one thing is of importance. Your sister has chosen the better part, and it shall not be taken from her."

Yeshua patted the cushion next to him and invited Martha to sit. She did, although somewhat reluctantly. Yeshua started his story again so that Martha could hear it too; indeed, I paid a little more attention. He told another story about a shepherd going after a lost sheep, and carrying it home on his shoulders, just as I had seen Yeshua carrying the lamb those many years ago in Nazareth. With each parable, Yeshua compared it to God going after the sinner and rejoicing when the sinner repented. My eyes were riveted on Miriam the whole time, for in many ways the stories Yeshua was telling were like her own. I could see they pleased her.

After Yeshua finished telling his parables, both my sisters got up and finished the meal preparation. We had a wonderful dinner and enjoyed great conversation. After supper, things got a little out of control, at least from my point of view.

We had no sooner finished our time at table than Yeshua poured some more wine for the women and sent them to the sitting area to "relax." The next thing I knew I was wearing a drying towel on my head.

"I wash, you dry," Yeshua said to me.

"What? I'm not doing women's work!" I said as I contested the very suggestion that I do the dishes.

"And why not?"

"Because"

"Because why?"

Before I said another word, I had a wet dish in my hand that needed to be dried. I reluctantly dried it and then another and another. I could hear my sisters giggling in the sitting room.

"This better not get back to the Temple. I'll be the laughing stock of the place for days," I said.

"I'll make sure it gets back to the Temple. I'm sure Caiaphas will want to speak to you about it."

"Not funny, Yeshua."

***

The next morning Yeshua departed with his remaining disciples. Yeshua indicated that he would teach in the small towns and villages on the way to John and Mariam's wedding and that he fully intended to go through Samaria. They were on foot, and the shortest distance between Jerusalem and Galilee was through Samaria. Yeshua did not see any problem with his chosen route. I of course did, but I kept my thoughts to myself.

We would leave the next day. I had an important chore to complete before our departure. I needed to choose our best wine for the wedding. My favorite part of running a vineyard is wine tasting. It takes years of experience to train one's palate to the finer aspects of wine. I could tell which side of my vineyard the grapes grew on. I knew my wine. One cannot rush wine tasting. It took me most of the morning to pick the three vats to take to Cana. Three vats would be sufficient to serve a hundred people, more than enough I thought.

I slept the afternoon away.

Chapter 21 A Wedding and A Sermon

I hired a donkey from my neighbour to haul our cart with the wine vats to Cana. I usually transported flasks of wine, so getting the vats on the cart was the biggest challenge. I quickly ascertained that my sisters were strong, for girls, and easily assisted me with the task. They were pleased with themselves.

The journey to Galilee was familiar, though nonetheless exciting and interesting. We made the usual stops along the way, with Arimathea being our first overnight stay. My sisters spent the night in the inn, while I stayed outside near our cart with the wine vats, our valuable cargo.

The caravan owner prepared a warm fire for his travellers as protection against the cool spring night. I lounged back and listened to the usual conversations about the Romans, trade, and complaints about the unusually cool weather. One man decided to change the subject matter completely; he asked, "Has anyone heard of Yeshua of Nazareth? A rabbi who teaches about the coming of the Kingdom of God, and heals the sick?"

I sat up and waited for someone else to respond. Someone did. "Yes, he was here in Arimathea just yesterday. He was at the Synagogue preaching when a man brought his son to him. An evil spirit possessed the man's son. This Yeshua you speak of, he drove the evil spirit out of the boy. It was amazing. Who do you think this man is?"

The first man spoke, "I don't know, but there are some who are starting to believe he might be the Messiah. He already has a number of followers. I'm thinking about following him myself, that is why I'm going to Galilee; I heard he is going to preach there in a few days."

"The Messiah? What, another one? Do you know how many men claiming to be the Messiah have come and gone?" Yet another man spoke up. "I'm not following anybody. Seeing is believing."

"What's your name, sir? The first man asked.

"Thomas Didymus."

"Well Thomas, come with me to Galilee, you just might see something worth believing."

"And your name sir?"

"Bartholomew or Nathaniel, I'm known by both. I'm from Cana."

I continued to listen to the stories about Yeshua; he was certainly making for interesting conversations and arguments among people. I stared into the fire wondering about my friend. It was apparent to me that Yeshua was more than a healer, the casting out of devils is something which lies in the realm of priests, not priests like me but special priests.

That night I slept uncomfortably on the cart between the wine vats. Martha's blankets kept me warm but the hardness of the cart caused my limbs to go numb. In a fitful sleep, I had a dream.

There appeared to be hundreds of people gathered around a man riding a donkey into Jerusalem. They were waving palm branches and throwing their cloaks down on the path before him. Shouts of "Hosanna, to the Son of David" rang out from the crowd. "Hosanna to the King of Israel,"

they hollered. I could not see who was riding the
donkey, the crowd was too great, it blocked my view.

Suddenly the scene change; I saw a man's head
bleeding from what appeared to be a crown of thorns,
this time the shouts were mocking him, "Hail, King of
the Jews." It was as though I was looking through a
veil that partially obscured my view. I could not see
the man who was at the centre of this torture.

Then, I saw a man carrying a crossbeam on his
shoulders, through the streets of Jerusalem; again, I
could not see who it was. I felt frightened. I could
hear the women crying. It was all a disturbing blur.

I woke from the dream shaking. I had no idea
what the dream was about or who was at its centre. I
laid on my back staring up at the stars trying to calm
my nerves. I prayed myself back to sleep.

***

We arrived in Cana the evening before the
wedding. Some festivities were already underway. We
met Mariam of Magdala's parents and the wine
steward, who happily took charge of my wine vats.
He indicated that he would store them in a secure
place for tomorrow's celebration.

The groom John bar Zebedee, Yeshua, and the
rest of his followers were having their own party in
Capernaum. They would make the short journey to
Cana in the morning. Martha, Miriam, and I found
comfortable quarters in the town's small inn. I was
exhausted from the lack of sleep on the cart. I drifted
off listening to my sisters' excited chatter about
tomorrow's wedding.

The local rabbi officiated the formal wedding
ceremony, which began late morning. Her father,

Simeon, presented the bride, heavily covered in veils, to the groom. The symbol of their marriage bonds was the tying together of the bride and groom's hands.

Martha whispered to me, "It's so wonderful to see two people who really love each other get married, rather than just an arranged marriage. See how happy they are."

The wedding feast itself was a great spread of food, served with my wine. I could see the wine steward happily decanting the wine from the vats into flasks, with which the servants then filled goblet after goblet. I glanced around the courtyard at the large number of guests. I estimated there were more than a hundred people there. I did a quick calculation, and began to wonder if the wine would last the entire meal; the servants were being very generous with the contents of the flasks and were going back to the steward for more. Yeshua's disciples were in a particularly celebratory mood.

Halfway through the meal, I saw the wine steward speaking with Simeon, Mariam's father. He looked concerned. I glanced over at the wine vats; a servant was standing next to them looking nervously into the containers. I was about to get up when I saw Myriam of Nazareth approach the servant. He nodded, and Myriam returned to her seat next to Yeshua.

I remained where I was, though I was somewhat on edge. A few minutes passed, and then I saw Yeshua get up from his place and go over to the servant by the wine vats. He said something to the servant. I continue to watch as the servant began to

E. Ann McIntyre

fill the vats with water. *Did Yeshua tell him to water down any remaining wine*? I was puzzled.

Yeshua went back to his place, and the servant scooped water out of one of the vats and gave it to the wine steward. I gasped. *What is he doing? The steward knows that it is my wine. What is he going to think? That I brought watered down wine?* I waited for his judgement, head in hands.

The wine steward said to Simeon, "Sir, most people serve their best wine first, and after the guests have had their fill serve the inferior wine last. You have saved your best wine for the last! More wine for all!"

I was shocked. The servant came and filled my goblet. I took a sip of the wine. I knew immediately, it wasn't my wine. I looked up at the servant. "Where did you get this wine?"

"Sir, I don't know. I put water in the wine vats," he said. "It just became wine."

I looked across the courtyard at Yeshua, who looked back at me and winked. I got up and went out into the street. Leaving the din of the festivities behind me, I sat next to the town well, where it was quiet. Once again, Yeshua had me perplexed, *how did he make wine from water, without even using a single grape?*

"My mother asked me to," his voice came from behind me. I turned around.

"How did she know you could?"

"She knows who my Father is."

Yeshua sat next to me on the edge of the well. "Are you mad at me again?"

"No, I've given up my father's fight with you. Next, it will be between you and Caiaphas, and I am staying out of that one."

Yeshua smiled and put his hand on my shoulder, "Wise decision."

"Yeshua, what are you doing? I've heard many stories about you. I heard you cast out demons. Is that true?"

"Yes"

"Why do all those people follow you? Who do they think you are?"

"You'll have to ask them."

"Some are saying you are the Messiah. Are you?

"I have come to bring the Good News to the poor, to set prisoners free, to heal the brokenhearted, to heal the sick, the blind, and the lame."

"What is your Good News?"

"Come to the hillside overlooking Capernaum tomorrow, and you can hear for yourself."

"Are you going to preach?"

"Yes"

I smiled at him and said, "You used to practice your teaching on me, so give me a preview."

Yeshua leaned back, looked at the sky, and closed his eyes. He took a deep breath and shared his teaching with me.

***

The next morning we made our way to the hillside, which overlooked the fishing village of Capernaum and the blue expanse of the Sea of Galilee below. By mid-morning, the people gathering to hear Yeshua preach had grown to five thousand or more.

Martha, Miriam, and I sat on our cart on a flat spot halfway up the hill. I looked around at the number of caravans present; it was clear people had

E. Ann McIntyre

come from great distances to hear Yeshua. To my left I could see a group from Jerusalem; I spotted Nicodemus and Simon from the Sanhedrin. Rumour had it that there was a group of Romans there including Claudia, the wife of Pontius Pilate, and Joanna, wife of Chuza of the Court of Herod. I silently prayed Yeshua would not say anything against Rome. It might get back to the wrong people. Roman soldiers, always present, hovered nearby.

Yeshua sat on the grass near the top of the hill, his disciples gathered in a tight group around him. Simon bar Jonah stood up and waved both his hands to silence the crowd. It became so quiet I could hear the birds chirping.

I looked around at the huge crowd; all eyes were on him. For a brief moment, he glanced skyward, his lips moving as if in prayer, and then Yeshua began to speak the words he had spoken to me the day before.

"Blessed are the poor in spirit, for theirs is the kingdom of heaven.

Blessed are those who mourn, for they will be comforted.

Blessed are the meek, for they will inherit the earth.

Blessed are those who hunger and thirst for righteousness, for they will be filled.

Blessed are the merciful, for they will be shown mercy.

Blessed are the pure in heart, for they will see God.

Blessed are the peacemakers, for they will be called children of God.

Blessed are those who are persecuted because of righteousness, for theirs is the kingdom of heaven.

Lazarus of Bethany

*Blessed are you when people insult you,
persecute you and falsely say all kinds of evil against
you because of me.*

*Rejoice and be glad, because great is your
reward in heaven, for in the same way, they
persecuted the prophets who were before you."*

I closed my eyes and listened, I felt his word
sink into my heart.

*"You are the salt of the earth. But if the salt
loses its saltiness, how can it be made salty again? It
is no longer good for anything, except to be thrown
out and trampled underfoot.*

*You are the light of the world. A town built on a
hill cannot be hidden. Neither do people light a lamp
and put it under a bowl. Instead, they put it on its
stand, and it gives light to everyone in the house. In
the same way, let your light shine before others, that
they may see your good deeds and glorify your Father
in heaven.*

*Do not store up for yourselves treasures on
earth, where moths and vermin destroy and where
thieves break in and steal. But store up for yourselves
treasures in heaven, where moths and vermin do not
destroy, and where thieves do not break in and steal.
For where your treasure is, there your heart will be
also."*

He set forth a challenge to us, his listeners, to go
deeper into our relationship with God and the people
in our lives. I got nervous when he told the people not
to be like the Scribes and Pharisees, to be humble, not
proud. I looked over at Nicodemus; he was nodding
in agreement. I relaxed.

Some of his words I had heard when we were
young boys in a nearby muddy pond, when he spoke

E. Ann McIntyre

to the Roman Centurion, "Love your enemies, do good to those who hurt you," and those words he said to me when we were older, "Consider the lilies of the field." It occurred to me that Yeshua had been preparing for this moment all his life.

I glanced at my sisters, tears were running down their faces as they listen to Yeshua speak. I looked around at the silent crowd; they too were in awe. There were many learned men at the Temple, expounding on the scriptures, but no one had ever spoken as Yeshua did at that moment. It was as though time stood still, allowing each of his words to sink deeper into my heart. Some of his words seemed in direct contradiction to the Law, but then he'd turn his own words around and say he was speaking of the very heart of the Law and the Prophets. I'd go from feeling great joy in my heart to starting an argument with him in my mind. I wondered, *Where did he get all this?*

Never had I heard anyone preach in this way. Yeshua offered a prayer, a prayer in which we all call God "Our Father." I smiled. Prayer should be simple with few words, but with deep meaning, *hmm maybe he has something there*. I thought. *He's going to have everyone calling God "Father."*

Several of the soldiers were sitting on their mounts behind us. At one point, during Yeshua's prayer to God as Father, I saw the Centurion remove his helmet out of respect, the other soldiers following suit. A thought filtered through my brain, *Maybe Yeshua is the Messiah and he will conquer Rome with his words.* I almost laughed aloud.

Chapter 22 The Anointing and The Wedge

Simon, Nicodemus, and Yosef were in a private huddle in the corner of the Hall of the Sanhedrin when I arrived for the weekly meeting. Caiaphas pounded the desk with his gavel and called the meeting to order.

Caiaphas began by calling into question the teachings of a wandering rabbi who was stirring up the people in both Judea and Galilee. He looked sideways at me. "This man's name is Yeshua bar Yosef of Nazareth. I want to know everything he says and does. Everyone and anyone who hears anything about him is to report to me. Do I make myself clear?"

Many in attendance nodded or shouted in agreement. I didn't. I couldn't see Nicodemus or Yosef, but Simon, who was directly in front of me, had his head down and arms folded inside his sleeves in disapproval. He was one of the oldest members of the Sanhedrin, he could get away with a slight disagreement with the High Priest, but I certainly couldn't. I felt Caiaphas' eyes burning a hole through me. I didn't dare look up.

It had been months since Yeshua had spoken his words on the hillside in Galilee. My sisters and I had left after he finished his teaching; we had to get back to Bethany. Nicodemus and Simon had stayed. There were more surprises from Yeshua after I left. People who came to hear Yeshua speak did not come prepared to stay very long. Many of them did not bring any food with them, and they got hungry. The way Nicodemus and Simon told me the story, Yeshua fed them all by blessing a few fish and barley loaves. He also went around the whole encampment healing people and driving out demons. Word of these things had made their way to Caiaphas and now, months later, he was seething. The people were paying more attention to Yeshua than they were to Caiaphas, and Caiaphas did not like competition. He was starting to see Yeshua as a problem.

After the adjournment of the meeting, Simon caught up with me and handed me a note. *"Come to my house two evenings after the Sabbath. I am hosting a private dinner party in Yeshua's honor. Do not tell anyone. This cannot get back to Caiaphas. Yosef and Nicodemus are coming. You may bring your sister Martha. – Simon"*

"What about Miriam?" I whispered to him. He gave me a hate-filled looked. Miriam's past hadn't been forgotten. I dreaded having to tell her she wasn't invited to the dinner for Yeshua. She would be heart-broken. *Why can't people forgive?* I thought.

***

I looked back at Miriam as she sat on her cushion with the dinner plate on her lap. Martha had prepared Miriam's favourite supper in a vain hope of cheering her up. I knew it wasn't working. I gave her a small wave as I closed the door behind me. Martha and I headed to Simon's house not far away, as he also lived in Bethany. I felt terrible.

"I haven't left Miriam alone since she came home," Martha said, "I hope she manages."

"Maybe Yeshua will come back with us to see her. She would like that. I didn't want to say anything to her, you know, get her hopes up," I said.

We arrived at Simon's house and were shown to our places across from Simon and his guest of honor. Yeshua greeted Martha and I with his normal brotherly hug. He looked past me with raised eyebrows; I shook my head and whispered, "She wasn't invited." Yeshua pursed his lips in annoyance.

Simon took the opportunity during dinner to ask Yeshua about his teachings. The conversation was going smoothly when there was a sudden commotion at the door. Someone tried to push their way in, and Simon's servant attempted to keep the person out. At first, we thought it was one of Caiaphas' spies, but then we saw a woman, heavily veiled; push her way past the servant and fall at the feet of Yeshua. I recognized the woman's clothing. It was Miriam. I was shocked. I grabbed Martha's hand, and we looked at each other in disbelief.

Miriam bent over Yeshua's feet and kissed them, allowing her tears to fall on them, and then wiped them with her long dark hair. She then pulled out an alabaster jar of our most expensive ointment and poured it on his feet. The aroma filled the room.

Simon was indignant. "Do you not know who it is who is touching you?" he asked Yeshua.

"Simon, when I came into your house you did not wipe my feet or pour oil on my head. This woman has washed my feet with her tears, and poured oil on me."

E. Ann McIntyre

"That's expensive oil, it could have been sold, and the money given to the poor." Judas Iscariot said.

"The poor you will have with you always. You will not always have me." Yeshua replied.

He reached down to Miriam and held her face between his hands. "This woman has loved much." Then, looking directly into Miriam's eyes, he said to her, "Your sins are forgiven you. Your faith has saved you, go in peace."

There was an audible gasp from everyone in the room. I was astonished. *Yeshua had just forgiven my sister's sins. How could he even say such a thing? Only God forgives sins. He was making himself equal with God.*

I sat back against the wall shocked at what I had just witnessed. Yeshua handed Miriam back the jar of ointment and said to her, "Save this for my burial."

***

Martha was brimming with joy as we walked back to the house. She had invited Yeshua to come with us. The two of them walked arm in arm up the street. I followed them. I was still pondering Yeshua's words of forgiveness to Miriam. I just couldn't accept that he had any authority to forgive sins. It was blasphemous of him to do so.

Miriam was home when we arrived. She walked up to Yeshua and politely thanked him for his words of kindness to her. The three of them stood together chatting about the dinner and laughing. I stood back. I wasn't feeling the joy, I was angry.

It was clear to me that Yeshua and I were growing apart. My sisters were becoming his disciples, they believed in him. I did not. It was a house divided. Yeshua was the wedge.

"The Lord Our God is One Lord!" it was involuntary, but those words came out of me.

Yeshua, Martha, and Miriam turned and stared at me. I said those sacred words again.

"The Lord Our God is One Lord."

"Lazarus, you speak the truth. Do you have something to say to me?" Yeshua stood directly in front of me.

"You cannot make yourself equal to God. Only God can forgive sins!"

"Lazarus, I…"

"Get out of my house!" I shouted at him, "Get out!"

"Shalom, I will not stay where I am not welcome."

The door closed quietly behind him. I walked over to it, grabbed it, and made sure it slammed.

"Lazarus, how dare you drive our friend out of my house!" Martha yelled at me.

"Martha, you don't understand…"

"No, no, I understand all too well, you cocky priest. You get out of my house, now!"

Martha went to my room and came out carrying my bedclothes and blankets. She threw them at me and ordered me to the roof, "Do try and stay warm up there."

I turned to leave and looked over at Miriam, who was crying. "It's my fault, it's entirely my fault." She ran into her room.

I went up to my old room on the roof. As far as I was concerned, Yeshua had stepped over the line by making himself equal with God. His words to my

E. Ann McIntyre

sister flew in the face of our core belief. I had to tell him so, didn't I? I was very much afraid the bonds of our friendship had snapped.

Chapter 23 Cold and Darkness

Bethany four months later

It was cold in my old room. The wool blankets hardly protected me from the winter temperatures, which had Judea in its grip. There was even snow on the hills around our home. I was still in Martha's cold grip. She fed me, washed my clothes, but that was it. I was sure she would mellow out after a few days or even a week after my outburst against Yeshua, but no, two, three, and now four months later, I was still in exile on the roof. She would not let me use the guesthouse in case "he" came.

"He", Yeshua, was in Galilee. Caiaphas' resourceful spies brought regular reports of Yeshua's activities to the Temple. They indicated he was living and teaching in Capernaum. Spring was bringing Passover, and that meant Yeshua would be coming to the Temple. Caiaphas was making plans for Yeshua's arrival back in Judea.

I wasn't included in Caiaphas' inner circle of planners. He still didn't trust that I wasn't in close relationship with Yeshua. Even so, I did not want any harm to come to him, so I was more than just a little concerned about Caiaphas' intentions.

I did have the opportunity to hear some of the details from the spies' report. Yeshua had chosen twelve men to be his closest followers. He called them apostles. The spies said they came from a variety of backgrounds. Yeshua had selected one of them, a man by the name of Simon Peter, to be their leader. I assumed it was Simon bar Jonah, the fisherman.

"Are any of these men less committed to Yeshua?" Caiaphas asked.

"We aren't sure yet. It is difficult to infiltrate the smaller group. Yeshua tends to take them off by themselves somewhere," one of the spies replied.

"Well, keep trying, it is important that we know exactly what he is up to. We can't have anybody claiming to be the Messiah, and rallying the people against us," Caiaphas said.

Caiaphas dismissed me from the room after that discussion. My uneasiness was growing. None of Yeshua's secret friends, like Yosef of Arimathea or Nicodemus, were in the room. I told myself I shouldn't care, but I did.

I left the Temple for home as snow was starting to fall on the city. The few flakes turned into a sizable snowfall by the time I walked up the hill towards Bethany. I turned around to admire how beautiful the snow made the city look.

It was the coldest month of the year, and I forgot to wrap my feet in cloths to protect them. When I reached home my feet were covered with snow and freezing. I opened the gate and promptly got a snowball in the face. Martha and Miriam were having a snowball fight and I got caught in the middle of it. We didn't get snow very often, but when we did people took advantage of it to have some fun. I decided to pay my sisters back for their attack on me. The game in the cold snow started to melt the ice between my sisters and me. They invited me inside the house. Just as I was going in the door behind my sisters, a snowball hit my back. I turned around to see who my assailant was.

"Gotcha."

I couldn't help but laugh and embrace him. "Shalom," I said, "It's good to see you."

"May I come in?"

Martha reached past me, and pulled Yeshua into the house, "Of course you can pay no attention to my brother."

I sat feet first in front of the hearth. Yeshua sat next to me. It felt good. Martha handed both of us a drying towel for our feet.

Miriam had disappeared; when she came through the door, she was carrying my bedclothes and blankets. Martha directed her to make up my bed.

"Am I staying?"

"Yes, but with conditions," Martha replied.

Wait for it. I thought to myself.

"First, you must apologize to Yeshua. Second, you must not speak ill of Yeshua and thirdly, you must help us clean up the dishes after every meal. Do I make myself clear?"

"Yes," I said.

Yeshua was grinning.

"Well?" Martha said as she motioned in Yeshua's direction.

I felt I could apologize to Yeshua without sacrificing my beliefs.

"I am sorry for my outburst the last time you were here. I assure you Yeshua, you are welcome here."

"Thank you, Lazarus. I accept your apology," Yeshua said as he reached out and gave me a hug.

"Good, now both of you eat your supper."

"Yes, Martha. Thank you, Martha," I said.

I didn't care about the conditions, I figured I could get out of doing dishes easily enough. The most important thing was that I was out of exile and in from the cold. I glanced over my shoulder as Miriam made my bed. It sure looked good.

Martha and Miriam excused themselves for the night, leaving Yeshua and I alone in front of the hearth.

"Shall we pray?" he asked me.

We knelt back on our knees facing Jerusalem. I led the recitation of the psalms. I still felt uncomfortable in Yeshua's presence. He must have sensed it.

"Lazarus, are we still friends?" he asked when we finished our prayer.

"It's hard for me, Yeshua, what you said to Miriam goes against my belief, indeed, our Jewish faith. You made yourself equal with God by forgiving her sins. You can't do that; you must know how offended many of us were."

"I can't change what is the truth."

"Yeshua, please don't say any more."

"Lazarus, I pray for you constantly. I know it is difficult for you. However, right now I am not asking you to be my disciple. What I value most is your friendship." His eyes were swimming with emotion.

I sat there for a few minutes not quite knowing how to reply to him. I valued his friendship too, but I knew that any relationship with him now could compromise my position as a teaching priest at the Temple.

"Can I sleep on it?" I asked him.

"Of course. I love you, Lazarus."

I stiffened as he reached out and squeezed my shoulder.

Lazarus of Bethany

"Shalom my friend, good night," he said.

Yeshua stretched out on a mat in front of the hearth. I went to sleep in my own room for the first time in four months. I stared into the darkness that surrounded me. My relationship with Yeshua wasn't fully restored. I couldn't give him the commitment he sought from me, not yet.

***

I was with my students in the Temple when it started. First, Chief Priest Ananias scurried by the classroom door declaring, "That imposter has done it now, wait until I tell Caiaphas."

"Who has done what?" I asked too late, as Ananias was already halfway down the hall headed towards the chambers of the High Priest. I poked my head out the door only to see a beggar being hustled down the hall by the Temple guards. I thought for a moment that the beggar looked familiar. It occurred to me that he was the same blind beggar who often stationed himself at the Temple gates. *What did he do?* I pondered. Next, another Temple official hurried by, announcing, "There's been a miracle at the Pool of Siloam, the blind man can see. That man Yeshua did it."

I should have known it was him. I dismissed my class and ventured out to the Temple's portico to see what was going on. Caiaphas and Ananias were right behind me.

"So, your friend Yeshua is back is he?" Caiaphas scowled.

"He healed someone. What's wrong with that?" I asked.

E. Ann McIntyre

"The man he healed is a phoney, he was never blind, so that makes your friend a fraud," Ananias said.

"That man was born blind, everyone knows that," I countered. "Ask his parents, they are right down there looking for him."

"Fine, we will," Ananias huffed as he stormed down the stairs after the beggar's parents.

They dragged the beggar's parents into the Council chambers where their son was held. I went down to observe the proceedings. Caiaphas and Ananias interrogated the man's parents until they were almost in tears. Finally, the man's father spoke, "I tell you, our son was born blind but now he can see. We don't know how that is, but it is."

The beggar and his parents were released. The beggar wanted to find the man who gave him his sight. I helped him find Yeshua, who was teaching near the Portico of Solomon. The man knelt at Yeshua's feet. They exchanged a few words out of earshot from me.

Yeshua caught sight of Ananias and Caiaphas; they had followed me. Their presence set Yeshua into a tirade, a scathing attack on Temple authorities.

He attacked all temple officials, priests, scribes, Sadducees, and Pharisees. Stunned by the ferocity of his words, I backed away from him until I was up against a pillar. I slid down the pillar to the floor. My head buried in my hands.

"You are like whitened sepulchres, all white and gleaming on the outside while being dark and evil on the inside."

I covered my ears, but I could not stop his words.

"Before Abraham was I am!" he shouted in response to Ananias' claim we were children of Abraham.

Then he said, "Moses longs to see my day." and "destroy this Temple and in three days I will raise it up."

I was writhing from a sudden pain in my right side. I was going to be sick. I held myself in until I heard his words.

"The Father and I are one!"

I was done. I retched and ran out of the Temple towards home. I held my stomach and shivered. I was hot and cold. My head was spinning. I struggled to put one foot in front of the other. Halfway home I collapsed on the road.

I felt myself being lifted off the ground. I managed to open my eyes slightly, I saw Philip on my left side and Matthew on my right. "We are taking you home." I couldn't even say 'thank you'. I passed out.

The dreams came back. The horrible dreams. A man was being beaten, scourged, and crucified. I couldn't get him out of my mind. I called out in hope someone would stop this madness. I was sick again. I tried to open my eyes. I couldn't. The dreams came again. I wanted them to stop.

The flagrum pelted his body. Relentlessly, the soldiers attacked him. This time I saw the man's face. Yeshua. I screamed, "No"

***

I could see Martha and Miriam attending to me. I looked dead. It occurred to me that I was looking down on my body and the whole scene inside the house. My sisters were weeping over my dead body. Miriam poured some of that expensive ointment over me. I couldn't feel it. I couldn't feel anything.

The scene below me grew dim. I was in total darkness. I couldn't see, hear, or feel anything. I could sense others. How I wasn't sure. I wasn't frightened. I was certainly curious. Was this death? I wondered. I didn't feel dead. Then again, I didn't know what it was like to be dead. If I was indeed dead, it wasn't so bad. It didn't hurt. I decided to pray since there wasn't anything else to do. I had my mind, or so it seemed. I was still me. Was I now in the Bosom of Abraham awaiting the Resurrection? Maybe. So, I called it my State of Waiting. *What to do? Pray? May as well.*

I tried praying the psalms, but my mind kept going back to that awful dream I had before I died, at least I think it was before I died. Hard to know for sure. Yeshua was being beaten; scourged. I prayed it wasn't real. I had left him in the Temple. I was hurting too badly, I had to leave. I didn't know what had happened to him. Had he been arrested at that moment? I wished I knew. I hoped my dreams weren't true.

I prayed some more. "*My Redeemer lives*", came to me. I prayed it again, *"My Redeemer lives."*

Martha's voice broke into my prayer, "*Lord if you had been here, my brother would not have died, but I know that even now God will give you whatever you ask."*

I thought Martha was praying. Then I heard Yeshua's voice.

"Your brother will rise again."

Lazarus of Bethany

Martha answered him, *"I know he will rise again in the resurrection at the last day."*

"I am the resurrection and the life. The one who believes in me will live, even though they die; and whoever lives by believing in me will never die. Do you believe this?"

"Yes, Lord," she replied.

I was puzzled. What was I hearing? Their voices faded.

Thud. What was that?

I heard Yeshua speak again.

He whispered, *"Father, I thank you that you have listened to me. I knew that you always listen to me, but I said this for the sake of the crowd standing around here, that they may believe that you sent me."*

There was a moment of silence. I listened. In the depths of my being, I felt his words.

"Lazarus come forth!"

I had to go. "Yes, Yes" I prayed, "I'm coming; I'm coming."

Suddenly, it was as though I was smothering, I had to get out, but I couldn't move. Bound head to toe, I squirmed and wriggled like a caterpillar, tumbling forward off a thin shelf; I managed to land on my feet. An incredible light pierced the darkness. I waddled towards it.

I heard another command, this time with my ears. "Unbind him! Let him go!" Hands pulled and tore at the bindings that enwrapped me. Freed, I tried to walk but my feet and legs would not move. I lurched forward and saw the ground coming up to meet me. A pair of strong arms and hands caught me. I looked up into the tear-stained face of Yeshua. He smiled at me and wiped the sweat off my face.

E. Ann McIntyre

Suddenly buried again, this time in the breathless hugs and kisses of my sisters, I struggled for air. Martha wrapped me in her arms while Miriam led me by my hands toward our home. People reached out to touch me, called my name, declared "It's a miracle." Between all the hugs and kisses, Martha whispered to me, "He came! I thought he was four days too late; you were dead." Her voice cracked with emotion as she repeated her words, "He came."

I looked back over my shoulder at Yeshua; he smiled at me and said, "I love you, Lazarus!" I did not need to ask why. We had been friends since we were twelve. What I did not know nor understand was the how. How did he reach deep into my death, into my State of Waiting, and give me back life? Yeshua was a rabbi and a healer, but this, this was different. This was incomprehensible. God alone had the power over life and death - a fact ground into me since I was a boy.

My body trembled. I knew the answer to my own question; I was a priest, a Levite, in the Temple for fifteen years. In my feeble mind, I dared to ask, *"Who is he?"*

Chapter 24 My Return

"Four days?" I repeated Martha's words. Apparently, I had been dead for four days, long enough to stink. I looked at Yeshua. I was confused. I had to ask him.

"How did you bring me back to life?"

"My Father heard my prayer."

"I heard your prayer."

Yeshua smiled and nodded. "Then you know."

"Know what?"

"The answer to your own question."

"No, I don't, I have no idea how I could be dead for four days, and then be suddenly alive again. Come on Yeshua, tell me."

"Do you believe?"

I knew what he was asking me. I believed he might have a special connection with God - that much was evident, even to me. However, beyond that. I didn't believe anything.

"I really don't know how to answer that question. I doubt that I can answer it the way you want me to."

I leaned back against the wall. We had a house full of visitors, all of them listening in on my conversation with Yeshua. I was reluctant to continue to talk about what I considered a private matter.

The door was open and I could see Caiaphas and his group of insiders hovering just outside our gate. I looked at Yeshua; he was looking at them too. I got a shiver down my back and a feeling of dread in my stomach. I wanted to tell him about my dreams.

"Martha," I whispered, "Can we have some privacy?"

Martha proceeded to tell everyone that I was tired and needed some rest after my experience. Our house quickly emptied. Martha closed the door behind her.

Yeshua and I were sitting next to each other. I had been dead. Now, thanks to him, however, he did it, I was alive and breathing. I needed to speak to him from my heart.

"Yeshua, I do love you as I would love a brother. I don't really need to know how you did it, how you gave me back my life, but I do need to say thank you."

Yeshua reached over and embraced me, "I love you too, and you are welcome my friend."

"I have to tell you something."

"Yes, what is it?"

"Caiaphas and the Chief Priests are plotting against you. I am afraid for your safety."

"I am aware of their plans."

"You have to get out of Jerusalem. I've… I've had some bad dreams. I didn't know at first who the dreams were about, but just as I was dying I saw who was at the center of those dreams. It was you. I saw you wearing a crown of thorns; they scourged you, and then crucified you. Yeshua, I'm so afraid for you."

Yeshua got up and walked over to the hearth. He threw a log on the fire, even though it was warm enough. "I know, Lazarus, I too have knowledge of the things of which you speak. But, I must live out the mission I have been given, even unto death, Pray for me that I will not do my own will, but the will of the one who sent me."

"Yeshua, you can't let it happen."

He paced the floor. I could see his clenched jaw ripple. His eyes fixed on the floor; sweat formed on his brow. He folded his arms inside his sleeves and looked at me.

"Lazarus, you must promise me one thing,"

"What's that?"

"During the next week, you must not go anywhere near the city. Those who seek my life also seek to destroy you, because your very existence gives witness to me."

"I don't understand."

"Caiaphas wants you dead, permanently. I need you alive. Will you promise me that you will not go to Jerusalem, no matter what happens?"

"Of course, I promise. I don't understand, but I will stay here if that is what you want me to do."

"Good. Keep your sisters safe too."

"I will."

"I must go now. Shalom, my friend."

"When will I see you again? Will you come here for Passover?"

"No, I will have Passover with my disciples," he paused, "in the Upper Room."

"In the Upper Room? Aren't you concerned that Caiaphas' spies will find you there?

"They won't. Not there."

"Will I see you after Passover then?"

He took a deep breath and nodded.

"Yes, after Passover, I promise." He tried to smile, but it was clearly forced; I could see the fear in his eyes.

E. Ann McIntyre

I still felt that dread in the pit of my stomach.

***

In the days before Passover Martha and Miriam were full of joy because I was back from the dead. Feigning that I was tired, and needed to recover from my death, I remained home and did not resume my normal Temple activities. This was a difficult thing for me, a priest, to do during the days leading up to Passover. Duty practically required me to be at the Temple. However, I had a promise to keep. I did not tell my sisters the full truth behind my staying at home. They didn't really care why they were just glad I was alive.

The surprising snows and cold rains of winter had given way to an early spring and bountiful growth in the vineyard. The vineyard was the best place for me to spend my time; I could occupy myself endlessly among the vines. On one occasion, Miriam joined me. She had learned well how to prune and was doing an excellent job. I appreciated her presence. Her quiet countenance complimented my need for solitude, without being alone.

"Lazarus, may I ask you something? Miriam said in her little girl voice.

"Yes, Miriam."

"What was it like being dead?"

"I'm not sure quite how to describe it."

"Did you see God?"

"No'

"Mother or Father?"

"No"

"Anyone?"

"No, there wasn't anything to see. I did sense some people there. Some were content to just be, others were in misery."

"How did you feel?"

"Content."

"Did you hear Yeshua call you?"

"Yes, I did."

"How did you come back?"

"I don't know. I just did. I felt pulled back if that makes sense."

"Why have you been so glum since you came back? Aren't you happy to be alive?"

"I... I didn't know I was glum. I have had a lot on my mind, Miriam."

"Are you worried they won't accept you back at the Temple?"

"I am concerned about how things will be when I do go back. Some of the leaders were not too happy with my return to life. So I am cautious."

"Why would they not be pleased? I don't understand."

"Only God has authority over life and death. What Yeshua did has stunned them and me."

"Are you afraid they might do something to Yeshua?"

"Yes."

Miriam took my hand in hers and kissed it. "Don't worry my brother; God will not abandon you or him. He did not abandon me."

She brushed a tear off her cheek. There was moment of silence between us. I had to ask her.

"My sister was... was it because of me?"

Miriam's eyes widened as her mouth began to tremble. She swallowed hard. "No, I...I felt as though

E. Ann McIntyre

I had done nothing for our family. I wanted to work, make Father proud. I don't know how it happened. I just…"

She turned and ran down the path to our house. I never broached the subject with her again. Not really something a brother should do I suppose.

***

The next day, near noon, Simon, the one who hosted the dinner for Yeshua, came to our door. He appeared stricken with anxiety.

"What is it Simon, please come in," I said.

He stepped in the door, took one look at Miriam, and said, "Can we speak outside?"

I stepped into the courtyard with him as he paced about. "Simon do you have something to tell me?"

"That man Yeshua, who apparently brought you back from the dead, paraded into Jerusalem today like a triumphant king, only he was sitting on the back of a mule. The people were singing his praises, and shouting "Hosanna, to the Son of David." They threw their cloaks and palm branches down on the ground before him. Lazarus, it was terrible. The people are starting to believe Yeshua is the Messiah, and he is encouraging them."

"I wouldn't exactly say he is encouraging them, he has never outright said he is the Messiah as far as I know," I countered.

"Nevertheless, he is dangerously misleading the people, don't you agree?"

"I suppose. Simon, I really don't know. Yeshua is not a dangerous person. He speaks of God with zeal. People haven't heard that kind of talk from anyone before. They are hungry and want to hear about the things of God in the manner in which Yeshua speaks. That very need says more about our failure as leaders of the people in their faith than it does about Yeshua's success as a teacher of the faith. He is giving them what they want and need to hear. We are not."

Simon shuffled his feet and rubbed his beard. "Well, I should have known you'd say something like that. He did bring you back to life. Shalom."

"Shalom," I said as I watch Simon open the courtyard gate and leave.

If Simon felt that way, I'm sure other people in the Sanhedrin had the same inclination. Things were getting dangerous for Yeshua. I wished he hadn't gone to the city. He may have convinced the people, but the leaders were another story. Their vehemence against him was growing.

E. Ann McIntyre

Chapter 25 The Arrest

It didn't take long for the novelty to wear off. Within a week, the story went from I was brought back from the dead, or maybe I wasn't really dead, just asleep and my sisters put me in the grave too soon. For whatever reason, people stopped focusing on me, which was just fine - except the miracle of it all was lost.

People were starting to say less than flattering things about Yeshua. One of Bethany's vocal opponents to Yeshua openly decreed in the town square that Yeshua performed his "so-called miracles by the power of the evil one."

Martha was shopping in the market one day for Passover spices when someone came up to her and declared that her whole family was possessed. She came back to the house in tears.

"Lazarus what are we going to do? It is as though the whole town is turning against us," she said.

"I'm sure after Passover it will all go away. People don't like things that they can't explain. I can't explain it to them. They just walk away from me shaking their heads."

"I hope things get back to normal soon. I can't even go to the market without people staring at me. I hear their whispers. Some say that I put you in the grave before you were dead. They are so cruel," Martha said as she wiped her eyes.

It was time to give my sister a hug.

I noticed Miriam, stone-faced, as she sat near the hearth. "Miriam are you all right? I asked her.

"I'm worried about Yeshua. They are saying awful things about him. That he hangs out with sinners and prostitutes - looking right at me as they are saying it. Lazarus, I think we are nothing but trouble for Yeshua. The things he has done for us are making it dangerous for him."

"I know. That is why I am not going to the Temple for Passover. I don't want my presence to stir things up in the Sanhedrin. Caiaphas has no patience with Yeshua, and I certainly don't want to give him a reason to go after him."

"I'm not going to stop worrying about Yeshua until Passover is over and he has gone home." Miriam declared.

***

I was not looking forward to this Passover, we were not going to Jerusalem and I did not expect anyone to be joining us. I made plans with the one neighbour, Jeremiah, who was still speaking to me, to celebrate the Passover Seder with his household. Jeremiah was an old friend of my father's and was always very supportive of us since Abba died.

Passover and the Sabbath fell on the same day this year, so people were rushing to get everything ready for the feast. Martha and Miriam were busy making the unleavened bread and the herbs and spice mixtures. I would bring the wine to our neighbour's home.

E. Ann McIntyre

It was late Thursday evening, somewhere between eight and nine; I was sitting out in the garden with several flasks of wine lined up for the taste test, when suddenly James bar Zebedee, Andrew bar Jonah, Philip, Jude and Simon the Zealot stormed our gate and landed in the garden in front of me. They appeared panic-stricken.

"What's going on? What are you all doing here? Where's Yeshua?" I asked them.

James was breathing so hard he could barely get his words out.

"They have arrested him," he said choking on his breath.

"Who has arrested him?"

"The Temple guards along with some Roman soldiers. They are taking him to Caiaphas' house for a trial."

"What? What trial? Caiaphas can't hold a trial in his house at night. It must be during the day in front of the whole Sanhedrin, and I haven't heard anything," I told them. "Are you sure it's a trial?"

"Yes, they took him and bound him."

"On what charge?"

"We don't know," Philip said.

"It's all very strange, Lazarus, the Master celebrated the Passover with us tonight- two days early. Only he changed the ritual meal. Oh, I can't say it…" James said.

"Tell me what happened? How did he change it? He can't change it," I said.

"I can't Lazarus. It is too hard to say... his body and blood…" James' words trailed off. I had no idea what he meant. They were obviously distressed, so I invited them into the house.

Lazarus of Bethany

Just as we were going inside Simon from the Sanhedrin opened the gate.

"We've been called to an emergency meeting of the Sanhedrin at the house of the High Priest. Are you coming?" he shouted at me.

I was frightened. *Oh, Adonai, it is true.*

"What is it about? What could possibly be going on at this late hour?" I demanded to know.

"They arrested someone on charges of blasphemy. Are you coming?"

"Who has been arrested?"

"A friend of yours, so you might want to be there." Simon had a smirk on his face. He turned to leave. I started to follow him. I stopped dead in my tracks. The promise I made to Yeshua not to go to Jerusalem no matter what echoed in my head. *What do I do? Keep my promise to him or go and try to help him?*

I stood for a few moments in the open gate. By this time, Martha and Miriam had come outside. Martha was instantly beside me.

"You have to go and help him. There are many in the Sanhedrin who hate him. The only friends he has are you, Yosef of Arimathea and Nicodemus. Please, Lazarus. Go!"

I didn't know what to do. He needed me. Years of friendship came down to this moment. I looked over my shoulder at his apostles who had taken refuge in our home. I wondered why they didn't stay with him. *Why is this up to me?*

"Where are Simon Peter and John? I asked.

"They went with him."

"Go, Lazarus, Yeshua needs you," Martha whispered.

E. Ann McIntyre

I turned to leave. Suddenly a huge flash of lightning came out of nowhere and struck the ground in front of me. It knocked me off my feet. I couldn't move as a strange pulse held me in place.

Martha screamed.

"Lazarus, are you all right?" she said as she rushed to my aide. I couldn't find my voice. The bright flash had dimmed my vision. I reached up to Martha who threw her arms around me and lifted me to my feet. Together we stumbled back to the house. I would not be going to Jerusalem. I could not help my friend.

Martha laid me on my bed and put cold cloths on my eyes and face. The lightning, the brilliance of which continued to dance across my eyes, blinded me. My hair and skin were singed.

The only thing I could do for Yeshua was pray.

Chapter 26 Grief

I spent the evening watching people move about our living area as though they were shadows on the wall. I tried to listen to the words of James and the others. It was as if they were speaking from the depths of the ocean. I realized that the lightning had affected my hearing as well. Even Martha's strong voice was like a whisper. Frightened by the experience of sudden loss of my eyesight and hearing, I was unable to participate in the discussions about Yeshua.

I could see the ghostly figure of Martha walking back and forth across the room. That was her habit when she was worried. She appeared to be having a discussion with another person who had just entered the house. I could not tell who it was.

The newcomer leaned over me and shouted,

"Lazarus, it's Thomas. The Sanhedrin convicted Yeshua of blasphemy. They are sending him to Pilate in the morning. They want him dead!"

I yelled out. "Nooo!" but I could hardly hear myself. I choked up. I sat up with Martha's help. I could not focus my eyes. I pointed to my ears, "I can't hear very well. Did you say that they want Yeshua dead?"

Thomas yelled in my ear, "Yes."

I leaned back against the wall. I felt helpless. I could hardly breathe. My dreams, my worst nightmares were about to unfold. Worst of all, I could

E. Ann McIntyre

not be there for him. He gave me back my life and he was about to lose his. *He does not deserve this. My God help him,* I prayed.

A thousand thoughts raced through my head. I thought *we could break him out of the prison before tomorrow morning and save him. There has to be a way of getting him out of this. Yeshua has done nothing to deserve death.* I had feared for so long that his way of speaking about his relationship with God would get him into trouble. I never believed it would come to this. My own thoughts were driving me insane.

"Peace my friend. Not our will but the Father's will be done." It wasn't my voice in my head this time. No, it was Yeshua's voice. I sat up.

"Is he here?"

"Is who here?" Martha spoke in my ear.

"Yeshua, I heard him speak to me."

"He is not here. You must have heard a memory."

I didn't dare say anything else. I knew I heard him and not in my memory. *Peace,* he said. His words did indeed bring stillness to my mind. I was in control of my thoughts. I laid back down on my bed. Martha covered me with my bed covers.

It was close to midnight when I finally drifted off to sleep.

***

Friday morning I woke before anyone else. I was still partly blind, so I fumbled my way to the roof, putting my hand on each stair as I went. I couldn't hear the sound of my own breathing - there was nothing but silence.

I knelt back on my heels and tried to pray the psalms, but my mind was filled with rage. I had to do something for Yeshua. I may have lost most of my sight and my hearing; I had not lost my determination to do the right thing. I had to get to Jerusalem and free my friend from the conniving grasp of Caiaphas. It was not yet sunrise. I could make it to Caiaphas' house before they took Yeshua to Pilate. I owed it to him.

I have walked the road to Jerusalem all my life, so I expected that I could walk it now without the aid of sight. I could see straight ahead but not much more. The light was beginning to fill the sky as I made my way past the Temple's Beautiful Gate and entered the city proper. Caiaphas' home was a few streets from the Temple. We occasionally held our priests' meetings there. It was a big house with many rooms and a large courtyard. I tried to think where Caiaphas would keep Yeshua. I was certain that there wasn't a prison in the High Priest's complex; however, there were some buildings at the back of the property. "*How*," I said to myself, "*am I going to get to Yeshua, there's no doubt that he would be surrounded by a number of Temple guards.*"

I felt someone touch me. I jumped back; I couldn't see who it was. "*Leave now, go back.*" I didn't know the voice I heard in my head.

"Who are you?" I asked.

"*I am one the Lord has sent. Go back,*" the voice said.

"I have to help Yeshua. I can get him out of Caiaphas' grasp before he is sent to Pilate."

Suddenly a force that I couldn't see pushed me back. It kept pushing me. "*This is not for you to do. Go back,*" the voice said again.

I was confused and frightened; I had no idea what was going on. Who, or whatever it was grabbed my hand, and started to haul me back up the road to Bethany. I had no choice except to follow. It continued to force me up the road until I reached the front of our house. Hands on my back pushed me through our gate and into the courtyard. Confused, I stumbled towards the door and pounded on it, "Martha," I called out.

The door opened and I fell forward landing on the floor.

"Lazarus where have you been? We have been worried," Martha said.

"I went to Jerusalem to help Yeshua but I was stopped."

Martha next words were not addressed to me.

"Thank you for bring my brother home. Who are you?" she asked whoever it was. I couldn't see anyone behind me.

"I am Michael. Please ensure your brother stays here. This is what the Lord wants."

I had heard the same voice in my head.

"Yes I will, Michael, but who are you?" Martha persisted in asking.

"I am a messenger. I must go now."

"Shalom and thank you," she said. I heard Martha close the door. She helped me to my feet and sat me down in the living area.

"Is everyone still here?" I asked her.

"We are here Lazarus," James said.

It occurred to me that I was hearing better. Martha put a plate of breakfast in my hands. I looked down and could see the plate of bread and fruit. Looking around the room, I saw the shadowy figures of the apostles, but I couldn't see Miriam.

"Where is Miriam?"

"I don't know. When I woke up this morning you were both gone, I assumed you were together. Was Miriam with you?" Martha asked.

"No, she wasn't."

I turned to the apostles. "Are any of you going to help Yeshua?"

"We don't know how we can. He is surrounded by guards," James replied.

"But you can't let them take him to Pilate," I said.

"Lazarus, there is nothing anyone can do. We aren't armed. We can't take on the Roman soldiers," Thomas explained.

I sat back hard against the wall and pounded my fist on the floor. "I can't believe this. Somebody needs to be with him."

"Peter and John are there, I think," Simon offered.

"We all should be there," I countered.

"I suspect that Miriam is with him. Where else would she be?" Martha said.

I put my hands to my face. I was worried. "I hope she is safe."

"I'm going to go and find out what's happening. I can't stand this any longer," Martha said.

"Can one of you please go with her?" I begged.

Not one of the men moved. They were too frightened to go anywhere near Jerusalem. *Cowards, the lot of them*, I thought.

"Don't worry Lazarus," Martha said as she put her cloak around her. I could see her wipe her face. She was frightened too, but that never held her back. *Please God keep my sisters safe.*

The door closed behind her. The room was dead quiet. There was nothing to do but wait.

Through my tunnel vision, I could see James' face. He stared blankly into the room, wide-eyed. His fingers fumbled a piece of bread. Mindlessly, he broke the bread with both hands and said some strange words. "This is my body." James bowed his head and wept. His whole body shook with emotion. I felt compelled to sit beside him and console him.

The day seemed to go on forever. It was still only morning, but with no word from Martha or Miriam, I was anxious. Things could not be going well for Yeshua or they would have come home by now. It was getting near noon. I could at least see the sun in the sky. I had no idea what was happening in Jerusalem.

My stomach was growling, but I couldn't bring myself to eat anything. The hours wore on. It was mid-afternoon when I first noticed the sun was no longer shining. It wasn't as though it was cloudy. It was a clear day, or at least it had been. I stepped outside. The light was very strange. It was getting dark. I glanced up at the sun. I could just barely see it. It had gone a blood red and it was getting darker.

I was afraid. I had never seen the sun go dark like that. I had heard of this kind of ominous sign, but I had never witnessed it. I went back inside and reported to the others what I had seen. They said nothing.

Suddenly I felt the earth shake. We all felt it. The sun was dark and the earth was shaking. It was terrifying. I fell to the floor and prayed. I thought we were all going to die. Within a few minutes, it all stopped. The earth stopped shaking and the light return to the sky. It was as though nothing had happened. I breathed a sigh of relief.

Another hour passed. It was getting near sundown of our Passover-Sabbath and Martha and Miriam had yet to return home. I had done nothing all day but sit in our living area with Yeshua's apostles. I was getting restless.

I heard the courtyard gate creak. I waited for the door to open. Miriam came in first; she was holding her alabaster jar of ointment. Her face was like stone.

"I didn't have time to anoint his body. They buried him before I could do it," she said.

"Buried him…" I couldn't breathe. My chest heaved. "What happened?" I shouted.

Martha closed the door behind her and sat down in front of me. She took my face in her hands, looked me straight in the eyes and said, "They crucified him."

I ran out the door and up the path to the clearing in the vineyard. I screamed and screamed and screamed at the sky. "How could you let them kill him? I hate you."

I hated God when my mother died but I got over it. I swore I would not get over this.

***

I laid on the ground for hours. I couldn't bring myself to move. I hated being alive. Yeshua told me that my being alive was a threat to those who sought his life. Yeshua was dead and it was my fault. They

E. Ann McIntyre

had him crucified because he brought me back to life. It was too much for their small-minded brains to consider that Yeshua was a special person sent by God to be with us. I still did not fully understand any of what Yeshua said and did. I just knew his life was over because I was alive. I hated myself.

It was cold that night but I didn't care. I wanted to die with him. Go back to the State of Waiting in the realm of the dead, where I knew he was. The Passover moon was bright. I laid on the ground staring up at the sky. I remembered the first Passover feast I spent with Yeshua. How he stayed awake all night in prayer while I slept on the roof beside him. I thought that perhaps I could stay awake with him tonight, the night of his death.

I gathered myself together and sat back on my heels, the way Yeshua often prayed. I had just a while ago told God I hated him. Now I was preparing to pray. I wasn't sure what to say. I couldn't even think of a psalm, so I knelt there in silence. Then I remembered the prayer Yeshua had taught on the hillside near the Sea of Galilee. That prayer, his prayer, suddenly filled my heart. I lifted it up to God. In Yeshua's words, I prayed.

"Our Father who is in heaven. Holy is your name. Your kingdom come. Your will be done, on earth as it is in heaven. Give us this day our daily bread, and forgive us our sins as we forgive those who have sinned against us. And lead us not into temptation, but deliver us from evil..." I started to weep again. I couldn't hold it in. I fell into a heap on the ground.

***

I'd have stayed there for days if Martha hadn't come the next morning and insisted that we fulfil our Passover responsibilities at our neighbour's house. I managed to get up and prepared to go the home of our friend, Jeremiah.

I picked up the flasks of wine, which were still lined up in the courtyard from Thursday evening. Yeshua's apostles, now leaderless, had left our home. Martha said James had decided we had given them more than enough shelter. She did not know where they had gone.

I went through the motions of preparing for the Passover Seder. I felt numb inside. I did not know what to tell our host. I wasn't sure Jeremiah would even care about Yeshua's death. I knew he had met him the day Yeshua brought me back to life. I decided it was best to keep my grief hidden as best I could.

Martha and I went to the Passover Seder as planned, but Miriam was too grief-stricken to even come out of her room. Jeremiah and his family received us warmly, expressed condolences at the loss of our friend. I was pleased for I knew their greeting was genuine. It made sharing the Passover meal with them a little easier.

My heart was a bit lighter after the Seder and I didn't hate myself; God, well I hadn't quite come around to Him yet. Yeshua's prayer was still in my head. Addressing God as "Father" was beginning to wear down my anger at him.

I went to sleep on my cot feeling at peace. I didn't know why I was at peace, but the war of words in my head had ceased.

Chapter 27 Adonai

The First Day

My eyes opened well before sunrise. I heard someone in the living area outside my bedroom. I got up to see who it was.

"Miriam, where are you going at this hour?"

"I'm meeting Mariam of Magdala and her friend Joanna at the Master's tomb. We are going to properly prepare his body which we weren't allowed to do on Friday."

"Do you need me to go with you?"

"It's not something a man should do. I'll be fine."

"Please be careful. Leave immediately if there is anyone around watching you. We don't want any more trouble."

"I will. I'll be back soon."

Miriam left carrying her alabaster jar of ointment. Martha was still sleeping, so I decided to go up to the clearing in the vineyard to pray. It would soon be sunrise.

***

The morning was clear and the full moon was just setting behind Jerusalem. As I leaned back on my knees, there was a slight earthquake. The shake slowly grew in intensity. I stayed down and put my hands on the ground. A bright light pierced my eyes; it seemed to come from the direction of Jerusalem in the west. I was frightened. I closed my eyes and bowed low to the ground. I didn't know what was happening.

Suddenly in my mind, I could hear music, wonderful music. A chorus sang out the words I heard before Yeshua called me to come out of the grave. They sang "*I know that my Redeemer lives and that in the end, he will stand upon the earth. And after my skin has been destroyed, yet in my flesh, I will see God.*" followed by great rounds of "*Alleluia.*" It was so beautiful. The fear left me. I was almost joyful. The singing continued, I didn't want it to stop.

I heard a voice call my name. "Lazarus."

"Shish, I'm listening to beautiful music," I said to whoever was trying to interrupt the singing.

"Lazarus, open your eyes," The voice said again.

"No, I don't want it to stop."

"Lazarus, it's me."

This time I recognized the voice. *It couldn't be; Yeshua is dead.* I opened my eyes. I was looking straight into the eyes of my friend. He was alive. I just sat there staring at him. He put his arms around me. I grabbed him. I could see the nail wounds in his hands and feet. I felt him, he was solid not a ghost. I started to weep, not from sadness but out of pure joy.

"Now do you know who my Father is?" he asked me.

I answered him from the depths of my soul. I spoke the words to him I never expected to say to any man.

"Adonai, Adonai," I said as I bowed before him and kissed his wounded feet.

"I love you, Lazarus. I have longed for this day."

My belief system crumbled. I held on to the man I had known for so many years. I knew my friend was also my God. Yeshua held me tight. He knew what I was going through. He helped me to my feet and said a most natural thing to me.

"Do you want to pray the morning antiphons together?"

"Yes Lord, I do."

We stood together in the light of a new day, faced Jerusalem, and prayed. I was in ecstasy. We were standing on the spot where Yeshua told me those many years ago that Yosef was not his father. Visions of our life together as friends flashed through my mind. The muddy pond, the first swimming lessons, the water into wine, saving my sister from being stoned to death, forgiving her sins, and most of all, bringing me back to life. How stupid and stubborn could a man be? I was humbled.

"Lord, please forgive my disbelief. I can't imagine what I put you through for so long. You had to die and resurrect before I would believe in you."

My Lord smiled, "Faith is a gift, an invitation. I'm glad to have you as a believer and as my friend."

"Thank you, Lord."

"Let's go and see if Martha is awake yet," he suggested

"Miriam has gone to your tomb," I told him.

"I have messengers there to tell the women that I have risen. Miriam will be back shortly."

We walked arm in arm down the path to the house. As we got to the courtyard, the gate suddenly flung open. It was Miriam and she was yelling at the top of her lungs. "Lazarus, Martha, Yeshua has…" Then she saw him.

"Master… "

Miriam threw her arms around Yeshua's neck. I grabbed her alabaster jar. I heard the door open. The Lord suddenly had two women wrapped around him. He lost his balance, and down he went.

Amid the laughter, I pulled my sisters off him and helped him to his feet. We were all in hysterics. Martha, ever Martha, managed to catch her breath and invite us all in for breakfast.

"I can always eat." The Lord said.

***

We lounged on the cushions as we ate. Our home was a joyous place to be. His death had been devastating for us and now we were sharing a meal with our risen friend. I was still trying to wrap my mind around it all. I was a priest; I needed to ponder, to understand what I was witnessing. Martha just talked and talked. Miriam was a virtual waterfall of tears. She had witnessed his crucifixion, and now his resurrection. She had been holding it all in. Now it was pouring out of her. Miriam had a firm grip of the Lord's hand.

The Lord was quietly enjoying our joy. He ate Martha's cakes with his free hand. He cleared his throat to speak to us.

"Your lives are about to change forever," he began, "You will all have to leave Bethany – immediately."

"Lord, what's wrong?" I asked.

"Those who sought my life will now seek yours, Lazarus. It is not safe for any of you to be here."

Martha and Miriam gasped.

E. Ann McIntyre

"Where shall we go Lord, this house and the vineyard are all we have," I said to him.

"It will not be easy. I know that this is where you grew up. However, it is imperative that you leave. For now, you can stay with my apostles at the Zebedee house. Caiaphas and his cohorts do not know it is our place of refuge."

"When should we go, Lord?" Martha asked.

"After darkness tonight. Take only what you need to live. I will tell you where you are to journey later."

"Yes Lord," we said in unison.

The urgency of the Lord's command sent shockwaves through us. This was Martha's house; we have lived here all our lives. Now we had to leave, my life was at stake.

Chapter 28 The Upper Room

I kicked the dust beneath my feet as I walked the well-worn path through the vineyard. The thought of leaving years of my father's labour and mine behind was painful. The vineyard was my life's work and my only source of income. The vineyard had supported my family for almost sixty years. It was hard to leave it.

Mindlessly, I fingered the vine branches and snapped bits of vine that I could see needed pruning. I continued to walk the path between the vines until I came to the clearing where I had encountered my risen friend. I should be joyful, but his imperative message that we leave this place weighed on my mind. I knew my life as a priest at the Temple was over; at least as long as Caiaphas was alive.

I left the vineyard and never looked back.

***

Martha came into the courtyard with a sad face; she had just delivered the Writ of Ownership of the house to Jeremiah and his family. They would not take it without paying for the house and the vineyard. Martha handed me half of the money they gave her. I was surprised at their generosity. It would be enough to support us for a while.

E. Ann McIntyre

Miriam was busy cleaning the house. She had her small haversack packed. She was ready to go. She was humming a happy tune.

"Are you two ready?" Miriam asked.

"Yes, we are."

"You are so sad; you'd think that Yeshua was still dead. He has risen! He is calling us to go on a journey with him. How can our life here be more important?"

Martha and I laughed. She was right. We would see him later this evening. We had a secret. The Lord had risen. He had changed our lives forever; that should be our focus, not our property.

I took one last look around my room to see what else I needed to pack. My eyes fell on the model of the Temple Yeshua had made for me those many years ago. It was impossible to take with me. It was far too big to carry. I crouched down beside it. He had put so much work into it. I felt bad having to leave it. I hoped Jeremiah's family would have some appreciation for it. I left my room, closing the door on the only life I had ever known.

***

It was after sundown when we left our house for the last time. Miriam led us, carrying a small oil lamp to light our path as we made our way down the road to Jerusalem. The only people out were the Roman soldiers who looked down on us from the city ramparts. The light from the torches on the walls lit up the soldiers' faces. They didn't say anything to us. Apparently, two women and a man walking in the dark wasn't a reason for issuing any alerts.

The air was cool and the city of Jerusalem was quiet. Most of the Passover pilgrims had already left the city or were staying at inns for the night. The city stillness was a surprise to me. I made frequent checks over my shoulder to ensure no one was following us, but we were alone on the street.

As we reached the Zebedee house, I glanced at the shuttered windows on the first and second floors; they appeared locked. Miriam tapped on the door and in a loud whisper announced our presence. There was no response, so she tapped again and spoke a little louder. I could just barely hear the voice from the other side of the door. Miriam responded in the affirmative. The door opened.

James ushered us in with a lot of 'shishing.' He wanted to know what had brought us to the house. We told him that the Lord had sent us. That he had visited us. James was dumbstruck.

"What do you mean? You saw him?"

"Yes. He came to me this morning just before sunrise. He had breakfast with us. He told us to come here, that we could stay here for safety. My safety to be exact," I told him.

"Well, I... Mariam of Magdala said she saw him too. He told her to come here and tell us that he had risen. We didn't know what to believe. Peter and John went to the tomb and found it empty, but they didn't see him."

"He has risen. He said he would come here this evening." Martha said. "So we expect he will."

Martha and Miriam headed up the stairs to the Upper Room. I stayed downstairs with James, who was in obvious distress.

"What's the matter, James?" I asked him.

E. Ann McIntyre

"Why would he come to you and not to his apostles? I don't understand."

"I can't answer that, except that he was very concerned about my safety. He said that those who sought his life were also seeking mine. He wanted me to come here tonight. He said I would be safe here."

"Well come upstairs, that's where everybody is," he said.

***

The Upper Room was dimly lit and crowded. Martha and Miriam sat next to Yeshua's mother and were engaged in animated conversation with her. John was listening in with a broad grin on his face. Mariam of Magdala was nodding excitedly as Martha and Miriam recounted having early morning breakfast with the Lord.

I glanced around the room to see who else was there. Simon Peter was in a corner of the room by himself, eyes fixed on the women chatting. James was pacing the floor in the serving end of the room. Salome was preparing supper nearby. All of the other apostles lounged on cushions scattered on the floor. Floor space was at a premium. John waved to me to sit beside him. I gingerly made my way over a few sleeping bodies.

"You saw him!" John whispered to me.

"Yes. He is very much alive. He said he will come here this evening."

John covered his face with his hands. I knew he was hiding tears. "I saw him die. I saw what they did to him. This news is so wonderful, I can't tell you what it means to me."

I reached out and put my arm across his shoulders. I looked over at Yeshua's mother Myriam; her eyes were swimming. She leaned against the wall and looked up, lips moving in prayer. John said, "She was there too. She saw it all. And so did your sisters."

Martha excused herself and went over to help Salome with the supper preparations. There were many mouths to feed and we just added to the numbers. Martha had had the forethought to bring food with us.

Just as the meal was about to be served, a knock on the door echoed up the stairs. Everyone sat up and looked startled. James went to the top of the stairs and listened.

"Is it the Master?" Andrew asked.

James shook his head and disappeared down the stairs. We could hear quiet voices conversing below us. Yosef of Arimathea and Nicodemus appeared, happily declaring that they had seen the Lord and that he had risen. Two more witnesses. The excitement in the room was palpable.

"Well one priest and two Pharisees can't be making this up," Philip declared.

"What about us; we women saw him too. He sent me to tell you. And you didn't believe me," Mariam of Magdala said.

No one gave her a reply. It was a simple fact. The witness of a woman was not to be believed until a man provided confirmation, which Yosef, Nicodemus, and I had just done.

***

E. Ann McIntyre

We finished eating supper and continued our conversation about the Lord. The women were in the kitchen area cleaning up from the meal. Suddenly a radiant light filled the room. Yeshua, the risen Lord, was standing in our midst. There were gasps and open mouths all around.

"Peace be with you," he said.

James was the nearest to the Lord. He offered James his hands to touch, to feel that he was indeed physically alive. He was not a ghost. James knelt and kissed the Lord's wounded feet. The tears streamed down his face.

The Lord moved around the room greeting everyone. He laid his hands on the head of each person saying "Peace be with you." I noticed that Simon Peter was moving away from the Lord, shifting further back into the corner as the Lord approached him. I had no idea why Simon Peter was doing this; I would have thought that he would move closer to the Lord if anything.

The Lord hesitated before approaching Simon Peter. "Shalom, Peter," He said holding out his hand to him. Simon Peter took the Lord's hand briefly, barely looking up as he did so. Simon Peter's face was beet red. I looked at John who raised his eyebrows but said nothing.

Next, the Lord approached our group. John could barely contain his excitement, although he did the courteous thing and stepped aside to allow the Lord to greet his mother first. The Lord held his mother close for a moment and kissed her head. Myriam ran her fingers down Yeshua's face and wiped his forehead, which bore the wounds from the crown of thorns. Neither one said a word. Myriam clasped Yeshua's face between her hands and kissed his nose. It was a tender moment between mother and son. There were many watery eyes in the room.

The Lord turned his attention to his youngest apostle, his eighteen-year-old cousin John. My sisters told me that John was the only one of the Twelve who stayed with the Lord until he died. John melted in the Lord's arms. I was looking at the Lord's face as they held each other. There were tears in his eyes. He was grateful to his young, bold, and brave apostle. They exchanged a few private words.

I thought back to the Dedication day when I put baby John into Yeshua's arms and John punched Yeshua's hand. That is when Yeshua's gave John the name 'Son of Thunder.' Even before Yeshua formally began his ministry, John was a believer. It took me, one of his oldest friends, a lot longer.

He greeted me on his way to the kitchen, "I'm so glad you are here. I will speak with you later."

The Lord went to the women in the kitchen. His aunt Salome was the first one he greeted. Throwing his arms around her, he said,

"I'm hungry, Aunt Salome. Do you have anything to eat?"

Salome gave her nephew a big hug as the Lord Yeshua wiped the tears from her cheeks. "Yes I have some fish and biscuits, just sit down and I'll bring them to you," she said. He grabbed a biscuit from the plate and made off with it, just missing a slap from Salome. That brought laughter to the room.

After greeting the rest of the women, the Lord sat down on the cushions in the eating area. We all sat down with him as he ate his supper. It was amazing really, there wasn't much talking; we were all just so thrilled to have him with us again, the how's and why's didn't matter.

Philip sat down beside the Lord, eyes wide, hand on the Lord's arm. "Lord, has the time come? Are you going to restore the kingdom to Israel?"

We all wanted to hear the Lord answer. I leaned in closer to him as he finished his last bite of fish and wiped his mouth.

"It is not for you to know the day or time that the Father has decided of his own authority, but you will receive power when the Holy Spirit comes on you, and then you will be my witnesses not only in Jerusalem but throughout Judea, Samaria, indeed to the ends of the earth."

After he said this, he called John, Mariam of Magdala, Yosef, Nicodemus, my sisters and me to join him on the roof. I thought we were going to pray.

Chapter 29 The Call

Since that first Passover feast when I first met Yeshua bar Yosef of Nazareth, I had always thought of this rooftop as ours. Tonight, however, I was sharing it and him with six other people. We were all curious as to why he invited us up there with him.

The Lord walked to the edge of the roof and leaned up against the half-wall staring at the Temple. He had his back to us for a few moments. He turned and looked at us standing there waiting for his words.

"All my Apostles will take my words to the ends of the earth; you, however, will take my Gospel to generations hence. You will not taste death until the Son of Man comes to his kingdom."

We all nodded. It was uplifting to know that I would share in spreading his words to many people. I felt a great sense of belonging to this select group - although I had no idea what exactly such a mission would entail.

The Lord extended his arms and invited us to move into a closer group around him.

"What I am about to tell you, you must not reveal to anyone. There will be five other people joining you. They will come in time. I ask all of you to give John clippings of your hair and fingernails. John, I will tell you what you are to do with these items. In time, I will reveal your presence to the world, until then you are to abide in secret. You will each have your own mission until I call you to come

203

E. Ann McIntyre

together. You will be the last of those who knew me on this earth. It is important that you remain close to me. It will not be easy. The road ahead will seem endless and difficult - do not lose hope.

Remain here in Jerusalem until the Spirit comes down on you from above. Learn from each other all that I have revealed to you. Keep in my love."

The Lord went to each of us and laid his hands on us. Then we rejoined the others downstairs.

***

It was difficult to keep quiet about what the Lord said to us. James prodded me, "What happened up there? What did he tell you?"

I made sure I didn't take a sleeping spot near him. Peter stayed in his corner. He never venture out even to speak to the Lord. Philip and Matthew eyed me hoping I would say something.

The Lord stayed with us that night, settling down on a mat near his mother after my sister Miriam gave him a masage using her oils. When Miriam started to masage the Lord, we all gasped at the lash wounds on his back. He assured us they no longer hurt. He never moved after that. His mother smiled and covered him as if she was tucking her child into bed – as she was, I suppose.

I watched him for a while, trying to understand why what happened to him was the way it was supposed to be. I looked over at Yosef and Nicodemus. I wanted to talk to them about what they knew of the Messiah. Did they have any clearer understanding of all this than I did? My questions would have to wait. The last few days had been exhausting for all of us. I knew I needed to follow the Lord into the land of sleep.

We were at peace. At least for now.

***

Clip-clop, clip-clop. The sound of horses outside the house echoed off the buildings and through the closed shutters. It was hard to tell what time of day it was with the room in darkness. The shutters did not allow much daylight to filter through the slats.

I rolled over on my back and saw the Lord Yeshua peering through the slats. He had a bit of a smile on his face. The *clip-clop* had stopped at the house. I thought that it couldn't be too alarming or the Lord would have warned us. I continued to watch his face as he looked out at whatever was transpiring below.

There was a knock on the door.

"This is Pontius Pilate, my son is with me and he would like to speak to Yeshua of Nazareth if he is here. We mean no harm to anyone."

Everyone in the room was suddenly on their feet scared to death. The Lord just looked at us and smiled.

"How does he know you are here?" I whispered.

The Lord put his finger to his lips, continued to look out between the slats, and even enlarged the opening.

"Mother, would you go down and speak with them? It's young Pilo's birthday."

Myriam nodded and slipped down the stairs. I thought, *Good grief he is crazy. He is sending his mother down to talk to the man who crucified him.*

E. Ann McIntyre

I heard voices from below although I could not make out the conversation. The Lord's smile grew broader as he gave a little wave to someone out there. I was certain Pontius Pilate was about to storm the house. I squeezed into the far corner of the room with everybody else. Simon Peter had company. He was not pleased.

Clip-clop, Clip-clop. The horses moved on, taking their riders with them. Myriam came up the stairs and said to her son, "I wished Pilo a happy birthday. Pilate said that they would find your body and return it to me. I wished them "Shalom."

"Ah, so he thinks my body has been stolen, does he? Well, I'll have to appropriately inform him otherwise," the Lord said.

"What?" I said, "What are you going to do?"

The Lord just smiled.

"But he asked for you when he knocked, why?" James asked.

"Pilo knows what my Father has revealed to his mother, Claudia. Pilate only knows what his Chief of Staff has told him. Pilate has been lied to, but he will soon know the truth," the Lord said.

"But Lord he killed you… you can't just go and make friends with him." I said.

"Lazarus, do you remember what I said to the centurion that day in the muddy pond?"

I shook my head. That was so long ago.

"Think about it… try to remember. It is important."

His words came to me, "*Love your enemy. Do good to those who hurt you.*"

"That's right. This day Pontius Pilate will know the truth and the truth will set him free."

Lazarus of Bethany

"Lord, perhaps we should all go with you in case he tries to crucify you again," I said, trying to sound braver than I really was.

The Lord shook his head at me.

He vanished. It startled me when he did that. He was not a ghost, I knew that, but he could vanish like a ghost. The Lord's resurrection was different from mine - I couldn't vanish. Everyone in the room took a deep breath.

There was another knock on the door. This time, I was close enough to the shutter to look out and see who was there.

"It's Thomas," I said.

James headed downstairs to let Thomas in. I could hear the excited talk as they came up the stairs.

"Alive?" Thomas was saying, "What do you mean he is alive? That's impossible. Dead is dead."

Thomas looked at me. I smiled at him. "Well, Lazarus is an exception. The Master is dead."

I thought I should try to convince Thomas. "I saw him first at our house in Bethany yesterday morning, and then he came here. He was with us until a few minutes ago."

"I didn't see him leave and I was outside on the street," Thomas said.

"No he didn't leave via the street, he just vanished," I told him.

"Oh, sure he just vanished," Thomas smirked.

I realized that if someone hadn't seen the risen Lord, what I was saying did sound preposterous.

"I tell you what. I'll believe your stories only if I see him and I can put my fingers on the wounds on his feet and hands, and I can put my hand in his side," Thomas said. He then saw the Lord's mother.

E. Ann McIntyre

"I'm sorry Myriam. I don't know what kind of cruel joke these people are playing, but it is certainly not fair to you."

"It's not a joke Thomas, it is the truth. My son has risen." Myriam told him.

Thomas shook his head. "I can't... I can't believe that I'm sorry but I just can't believe it unless I see him with my own two eyes."

Thomas went back down the stairs and left the house. His disbelief didn't surprise me. I'd probably be the same way if the Lord hadn't come to me. I wondered how I could convince people who didn't know the Lord if I couldn't convince Thomas. It was then that I realized that the mission the Lord had given me was going to be difficult.

Chapter 30 Sent

The Lord invited his apostles to go back to Galilee where he would meet them. The rest of us remained in Jerusalem for the next week or so. I was housebound, confined to the Zebedee house for my own safety. Martha made the occasional trip to the market for food but kept herself heavily veiled so that no one would recognize her. We had to stay hidden until the Lord told us otherwise.

Yosef and Nicodemus stayed with us too. They felt it was unwise to go back to the Temple. Sad really, when I thought about it. They were two men of God who had dedicated their lives to the formation of young minds, teaching them about God, something they could no longer do in the Temple. They were followers of the Lord Yeshua now, and Caiaphas knew it.

Yosef filled me in on what happened the night of Yeshua's arrest. Judas Iscariot had betrayed Yeshua to Caiaphas' fellow accomplices. He wound up committing suicide. I suspected something had happened to him but I wasn't sure what. That was the night I couldn't hear all the discussions in our house after I was struck by lightning.

Then Yosef told me that Simon Peter, Yeshua's chosen leader of the Twelve, had denied that he even knew the Lord not once, not twice, but three times. No wonder Simon Peter could not even look at the Lord. He was ashamed. I understood what Simon

Peter was going through, but knowing the Lord, he would work it out. He never gave up on me.

***

Later that week, almost a week after the Lord's death, Thomas came back to the house looking for the other apostles. They weren't there, but Thomas decided to stay anyway rather than make the journey back to Galilee to find them. Thomas was convinced that the whole mission around Yeshua was "*as dead as he is*" - I believe those were his exact words. There was no point in trying to prove to him that he was wrong, that the Lord was alive. However, I tried, anyway.

"You are delusional Lazarus, it is because you were half dead yourself that you think the Master is alive," Thomas said.

"I wasn't half dead, I was totally dead. Moreover, I'm not delusional. None of us are - just ask Masters Yosef and Nicodemus," I shot back.

Thomas glanced in the direction of the two Pharisees and shook his head. "Old men can be mistaken too," he said. Those two '*old men*' rolled their eyes.

***

The day after the Sabbath, I woke up to what sounded like thunder on the stairs. I sat up with my heart thumping in my chest. I thought it was the Temple guards coming to arrest me. Instead, a jovial Simon Peter announced his presence in the Upper Room. The others, all eager to tell us what they had experienced in Galilee, quickly followed him up the stairs. Most of what I got from all the chatter was that they went fishing and wound up catching a net full of fish after the Master bid them to cast their nets on the other side of the boat - again. He had been doing that since we were twenty-five. Granted, I didn't believe it then, but by now I knew that Yeshua could convince fish to jump into a net.

I gathered from Simon Peter's newfound joy that he and the Lord had reconciled. It was soon obvious; Simon Peter was in charge of the group again. He asked me to drop the "Simon" in his name.

"The Lord calls me Peter and that's what I will be using from now on."

"Very well," I said.

Thomas seemed to be pouting in the corner, the same corner Peter had been crouched in a week ago when the Lord came to us. His eyes darted around the room, seemingly trying to reconcile the joy of all of us who had seen the Lord with his own assertions that the Lord was dead. Arms crossed, he sat back against the wall, eyes downcast.

The light of the Lord filled the room as it did a week ago. The Lord's bare wounded feet stood in Thomas' line of sight. His eyes widened, he looked up. His mouth opened. At the Lord's invitation Thomas crawled forward, he touched the Lord's feet and hands, and he placed his hand in the Lord's side. Thomas prostrated himself before the Lord - his words echoed through all of our hearts.

"My Lord and my God!"

"Thomas you believe because you have seen me. Blessed are those who have not seen but still believe," the Lord said. A small but significant chastisement,

E. Ann McIntyre

one I was familiar with in my own life. I certainly couldn't fault Thomas.

***

In the days and weeks that followed, we saw less of the Lord, but it seemed more people who had followed him for the last three years did see him. Reports came in from many of the towns and villages where he had preached and healed people. It was exciting. There was no lack of stories of his appearance. One thing was beginning to dawn on me; he was preparing to leave us – permanently. When he did come to the Upper Room, he talked about coming from the Father and now he must go back to the Father before the Holy Spirit could come upon us.

One day early in the morning, he appeared to us again. This time he invited us to follow him. I hesitated. He told me to cover up and come along; I would be safe. I joined the large group and followed him. The Lord too was well covered as we slipped out of the City gates and headed to my hometown. He led us out of Jerusalem towards Bethany.

The Lord led us up the big hill in Bethany where I had taken him when we were boys, the week of my becoming a Son of the Commandment. The Lord Yeshua went up ahead of us and stood at the top as we gathered around him. He spoke to us, "As the Father has sent me so too am I sending you. Go now and make disciples of all nations, baptizing them in the Name of the Father and of the Son and of the Holy Spirit."

After he said this, he lifted up before our eyes and disappeared from our sight. His messengers told us that he would come back in the same way we saw him go. At that moment, I felt like an orphan. I felt that I was just getting to know the Man from Nazareth, a person I had known all my life – there was so much I still needed to know, but he was gone.

We returned to the Upper Room with a mixture of joy and sorrow in our hearts. We would miss him. Peter counselled us to all wait together until the Lord sent the Holy Spirit to us. We passed the days in prayer, breaking bread together in the way the Lord had during his last Passover Seder with his apostles. We ate of his body and drank of his blood, which was one of the many things I didn't understand, but I believed it to be true because he said so. As a priest, I understood the meaning of blood sacrifice, only this time he was the unblemished lamb. It was a powerful ritual for me.

Peter asked me if I would like to share in the ministry of the Apostles and be able to lead the Lord's Supper and preach his Word. I was humbled. Peter laid his hands on me and anointed me with oil declaring me as a new kind of priest. I was the first one outside of the Twelve to receive this anointing.

The next time we celebrated the Lord's Supper, I broke the bread and spoke the Lord's words over the bread and wine. It was an emotional moment for me. I was only beginning to understand what the Lord was asking of me. I didn't feel worthy. I was one of the last to believe.

***

It was late spring and the crowds were gathering in Jerusalem again, this time for the feast of Pentecost, a celebration of the first spring harvest. It

E. Ann McIntyre

was a time when I would bring in the first grapes of the season, and make my spring wine. To me that was Pentecost.

We gathered in the Upper Room, which was getting over-crowded with the Lord's followers. He must have invited everyone he knew to join us there. The house, still shuttered, was dark and hot with so many people. I was flat up against a wall as we listened to Peter preach about the Lord's resurrection and his mission to the people of Israel.

Suddenly there was a great noise from the outside, like a windstorm. The force of it ripped off the shutters, allowing the blazing noonday sun to pierce the darkness of the Upper Room. A ball of fire came through the windows and hovered for a moment over the centre of the room. We were frightened. The women screamed. The fire then expelled small tongues of flame that hovered over the head of each person. The room fell silent.

I'm not sure if I can adequately describe the immensity of what I felt at that moment. The Lord was with me, in me, all around me. I felt as though I was on fire with every word he had ever spoken. I knew him at that moment better than I had ever dreamed I'd know anyone. I felt loved. I fell to my knees. I was in ecstasy.

The flames disappeared but the effects were just beginning. We had a mission, we had been sent.

Lazarus of Bethany

Part 2

**And know I am with you– Until the End of Time"
(Mt 28:20)**

Chapter 31 Adrift

Peter, James, and John preached the risen Lord's Gospel with great courage and boldness, thus attracting many new followers to The Way, as we called the Lord's mission. I knew that Jerusalem was the place for the Apostles to preach - the Lord had other plans for my sisters and me. It was getting time for us to move on, to take his message to other parts of the Roman Empire.

Shortly after the Lord left us, I stopped wearing my priestly garments. I knew I couldn't go anywhere as long as I wore them, so I took up wearing simple robes instead, an act which I'm sure brought a smile to my Lord's face if only I could have seen it. Martha had brought with her the robe Myriam of Nazareth had made for me years before. It still fit. It pleased Myriam to see me wearing it.

The Way was not without its persecutors. The Sanhedrin condemned a young follower by the name of Stephen and stoned him to death; an act approved by a Pharisee named Saul of Tarsus, a man determined to eliminate the followers of the Lord Yeshua.

Some of the apostles had already left Jerusalem for different parts of the world. They knew they would never return. Thomas went east. His plan was to follow the silk trade route wherever it took him. Philip went south towards Egypt. James was planning to head west across the Great Sea, but he never made it. He died at the hands of Herod. Herod also arrested Peter and John. They later escaped - somehow. Tensions were rising between the Jewish community leaders and those of us who were followers of Yeshua. Determined to rid Jerusalem of the Lord's message, the Sanhedrin leaders had thought that by killing him they would end his movement. They had no idea how strong the Lord made us. They could kick us out of the Temple, and local synagogues, but that would not stop us from preaching in his name.

In consultation with the church leaders, my sisters and I agreed to take the long journey to the westernmost region of the Empire. We would travel beyond Rome to a province we had heard visitors speak of - a place called Gaul. There were many Jews living in the area who needed to hear the words of the Messiah. The journey by ship would take several months. The money we had saved from the sale of the house and vineyard would be sufficient to get us there. The prayers and blessings from the Lord's community would guide our way.

Our mission began almost four years after the Lord's death and resurrection. We had our last celebration of the Lord's Supper with the Jerusalem church; it was our moment of missioning. We hired a caravan and headed for Caesarea. We left Jerusalem with some sadness in our hearts, but also joy as we headed into the unknown, taking the Lord's message with us.

***

I remembered the first trip we had made to Caesarea, the city by the sea, with Father. How much fun we had looking back at the City of Jerusalem. This time none of us looked back. We had heard the Lord's words given to us through his apostles, "*Once*

E. Ann McIntyre

you have put your hand to the plough do not look back." I put my arms around my sisters, and together we sang and hummed the psalms.

The further we got from Jerusalem the safer I felt. It was the last year for Caiaphas as High Priest, but in my gut, I felt he would not have stopped looking for me. As long as I was in Jerusalem, I never felt safe. As we neared Caesarea and its port of many ships, I was beginning to relax. We would leave the land of our birth forever.

Caesarea's white Roman buildings and fine Governor's Palace stood out against the blue sea. I assumed Pontius Pilate was in residence. He had not sanctioned nor pursued any charges against the Lord's followers in the years since he sent the Lord Yeshua to the cross. John even told us we had nothing to fear from him. Did the Lord really visit him that day after his resurrection? John either didn't know or wouldn't say. I knew Herod was the one who had cooperated with the Jewish leadership by ordering the arrests and deaths of members of our community, not Pilate.

We arrived in the Roman capital of Judea late in the afternoon on the second day of the week. We would have to hurry to arrange for a ship to take us to Rome, where we would then travel to the Roman province of Provincia, in southern Gaul.

I met with a shipping agent, who indicated a ship willing to take passengers would be departing early the next morning. They would provide us with joint quarters since we were brother and sisters, but they would not provide us with food or water. Martha and Miriam quickly located a market where they could get some provisions for the journey. We were all beginning to feel excited.

While the women were shopping, I found a room in an inn located along the boardwalk near the ships. It would do for the night. After we had our meal, we celebrated the Lord's Supper. I spoke the Lord's words over the unleavened bread and wine we had brought with us. We sang psalms and shared the Lord's message with each other. We decided that we should do this every day so we would not forget all the stories we heard from the apostles.

Late in the evening, we all felt exhausted from the long journey. My sisters went to bed; I decided to pray under the stars before turning in. I found a bench located just a few steps from the inn. It gave me a panoramic view of the harbour. Torches around the pier lit up the ships moored there for the night. There were a few people milling about. Most of the talk I could hear was about what ships were coming and going and what cargo they transported, there were no discussions about revolution. They were all Romans, or so it seemed.

It was time to pray, or shall I say, talk to my friend. He promised he would always hear us, and be with us until he came again. I closed my eyes and in my mind told him about our journey thus far. I was just about to finish with the Lord's Prayer to the Father when I felt someone close behind me.

"Lazarus?" a voice said.

I turned to see a Temple guard with a raised hand clutching a cudgel.

***

My head hurt. I opened my eyes, I was in a sack of some sort; I could breathe through the mesh. A rope gagged my mouth. It went down my back, wrapped around my hands, and then down to my feet.

I was in a boat that much I could figure out. I could hear the water lapping up against the sides.

Gagged, bound, and in a sack on a boat that rocked back and forth on the sea made me nauseous. I was suddenly sick. I couldn't breathe. With some effort, I cleared my throat. There was a little air coming through the mesh of the sack, so I pressed my nose up against it to breathe.

Was I alone, adrift on the sea, or a prisoner being taken somewhere? I couldn't hear any voices. I could only hear the water against the vessel pushing it, and me, further out to sea. I could see the sky through the mesh. It looked like a clear day. I could not see anything else. The sack I was in was getting hot as the sun approached its summer apex. It wasn't going to get cooler anytime soon. I fought the nausea, choked, and gasped for air. I feared I was going to die.

I thought about my sisters. Were they well? Had they also been taken? I felt tears well up in my eyes, I couldn't wipe them. They trickled down my face. *Oh Lord, is this what is to happen to me? The long arm of Caiaphas finally found me; determined to end what you started.* I felt helpless.

Somehow, in the rocking and rolling of the boat, I fell asleep. At one point, I woke and felt a terrible thirst. My tongue was raw and my mouth was blistering from the rope firmly in place between my teeth. It was then that I knew how I would die. My thirst would only get worse with the sun blaring down on me. I would bake to death in that sack. I prayed that the Lord would make haste to come and get me. I could no longer focus my thoughts. I passed out. I felt

Lazarus of Bethany

myself slip away. I looked down on the sack containing my body. I could see the vastness of the sea around me. I had been through this before; I was dead again.

I found myself standing in a vast vineyard that stretched out as far as the eye could see. The vines bore plump grapes ready for the picking. I felt light and happy. The oppressive heat and thirst were gone. I was free. I looked over my shoulder and saw my sisters standing near a house and waving to me. I started to run towards them…

Plop, plop, plop, flash, boom. I was startled awake by a storm and rain. I was still in my floating prison. The rain was soaking my sack and running down my face. Water, it was water for me to drink… I pressed my nose and mouth up against the mesh as hard as I could. It worked. The water began to run into my mouth, held open by the rope. It was just a trickle but it was water, and it was glorious.

The water was doing something else as it soaked through the sack. It was allowing the rope to stretch with each upward movement I made with my head. The rope in my mouth was getting looser. I could wiggle my hands in the loop behind my back. Finally, I managed to work the rope out of my mouth. It fell down my chin to my neck. It was enough to free my hands.

I pulled my hands around to my front and worked the rope off my neck. The rest was easy as I kicked my feet and the sack fell loose at the bottom. I kicked again and wiggled until I could pull myself out of the sack. The rain poured down on me. I lifted my head skyward, mouth wide open, praising and thanking the Lord for the rain, and for setting me free.

E. Ann McIntyre

I had only one problem. It was the middle of the night, and I was adrift on the Great Sea.

Lazarus of Bethany

Chapter 32 Rescued

The next day the waves battered my skiff. The water splashed against the sides of the boat and soaked me, and contaminated the rainwater in the bottom of the boat. I lost my only source of drinking water. I hunkered down in the middle of the boat as best I could. The strong winds continued late into the next day. I was scared, hungry, thirsty, and alone.

Occasionally, I sat up on my elbows and looked over the edge of the boat searching the horizon for a ship to rescue me, or perhaps land where I could go ashore; I could see neither. I laid back down and tried to pray. Nothing would come. I couldn't even put together words for my Lord, my friend. My mind was empty. It was as if I was already dead. I had no conception of time or what day it was. I had no idea how long I was on the water. I had a large sore lump on my head. I could only put cool water on it to relieve the pain. I needed help.

The next morning the waves were calmer. I could sit up and scan the horizon for something, anything that would help me. Sometimes I thought I saw a great island only a mile from me off to the left, but then the same island would appear on my right. I concluded I was hallucinating. A desperate mind will see what it wants to see, and I was getting desperate.

Another night, a cold night. I wrapped myself in the sack. It was wet and the wind blew right through it robbing me of any warmth. I drifted in and out of

E. Ann McIntyre

sleep. Sleep was the only escape I had from my dire situation. I dreamt crazy dreams. It was as though my mind was trying to be somewhere else, somewhere safe, warm, with plenty to eat and drink. The valley of the vineyard was a recurring dream. It was like home. I wanted to go there.

Suddenly something struck my boat. I sat up and held on to the sides as it shuddered. It was dark. I couldn't see, but I heard voices.

"Help me. Help I'm in a boat, help," I hollered.

I heard more voices, louder this time. I called out again.

"Help me please."

"Who are you?" What are you doing out here?" said a voice from above me. I hesitated to say my real name; I took my father's name.

"I'm Boethius. I was hit by robbers and set adrift. Can you help me please?"

Finally, I saw a lamp above me. I heard something bang down toward me. A man's face appeared next to the lamp.

"I have sent a ladder down to you. Can you see it?"

"No, I heard it though," I replied.

He held the lamp closer to the ladder. I could see parts of it. The ship was hitting up against my skiff. I tried to stand on the edge, but the motion of the waves kept knocking me back.

I stood on the edge again, reached for the ladder, and missed on my first attempt. I stepped back into the skiff. The ship closed in on me again. I made a leap for the ladder that I could not see. I felt it with my hands and grabbed hold. I hung there for several moments and tried to catch my breath. My heart raced.

I tried to get my feet on the ladder, but I couldn't find a rung. The sea was below me. My boat was gone. I had to go up or die. I looked up and saw the lamp. I had to climb towards it. My arms ached as my hands held on to the rope ladder. I finally found a foothold below me. I pushed upward, one hand over the other, I made headway on the ladder. I was exhausted. I thought my arms would come out of my shoulders. Everything ached. I continued to climb. Then I heard another voice.

"Pull the ladder up you fools."

I looked up and saw two more faces. They hung the lamp on the side of the ship and all three men pulled the ladder, and me, onto the ship.

I landed hard on the deck. Sore and tired, but glad to be alive.

***

As I laid on the deck, I looked up at my rescuers, barely discerning their faces. I recognized one of them. I was certain it was the physician Lucanus, who had come to our home to help with Philip during Pilate's bloody crackdown in Jerusalem. Lucanus nodded to me and put his finger to his lips. I tried not to show any recognition.

"Saul, perhaps we should take this man below deck, and I could treat him for his time at sea," Lucanus said.

"Yes, yes of course. Proceed. I'll talk to him in the morning," the man called Saul said.

I made a sudden realization. One of my rescuers was Saul of Tarsus. I'd never seen him before nor he me. He only joined the Sanhedrin in the last couple of

E. Ann McIntyre

years. I knew now why Lucanus warned me not to speak.

Physician Lucanus helped me to my feet. I was unsteady and needed to sit down for a few minutes. I was dizzy and weak. Lucanus asked the others to help me down the stairs to the lower deck. I could not make it on my own. Lucanus laid me down on a bed. The room was spinning, that's all I remember.

***

I woke up the next day with a cool cloth on my head and water trickling down my mouth. The physician sat next to me.

"How do you feel?" he asked with a smile.

"I'm feeling better thank you," I replied.

"Do you think you can sit up?"

I nodded and he gently helped me to sit, then handed me a cup of water.

"You need to get more water into you. If you can keep this down I'll try you on some hot soup."

I took a sip of the water. It went down and seemed to stay there. I took more. It felt good. I finished the entire cup. Lucanus waited to see how I did. We smiled at each other. He looked over his shoulder to ensure we were alone.

"Lazarus, how did you wind up in the sea?"

"My sisters and I were headed to Rome and Gaul; we were going to take a ship out of Caesarea. I went outside to get some air and a Temple guard struck me. I don't know what happened after that. I woke up the next day in the boat."

"Do you know who did this to you?"

"Caiaphas has wanted me dead ever since Yeshua raised me from the dead. And after his resurrection, the Lord warned me about him and his cronies."

"I was going to ask you about what happened to Yeshua. I witnessed his crucifixion. It was terrible. Then weeks later, I heard rumors that he came back to life. I didn't know if it was true. You saw him after his death?"

"Yes, I did. Why are you with Saul? He hates the followers of the Lord."

"He has a condition that requires medical attention. He hired me. I only recently became aware of his anger with Yeshua's followers. That is why I warned you not to admit you knew me. He might ask why."

"I got that from your demeanour. We will have to be careful. Where are you headed?"

"He is going to Laodicea and then to Damascus. He travels a lot. He doesn't tell me what he is doing. I'm his physician, not his confrere. Look, I want to know more about Yeshua if you would tell me. I won't tell Saul, I promise you can trust me."

"I can tell you as much as I know. We'll have to be discrete; Saul might be suspicious if we are together too much."

"You're right. I want to write down everything you tell me. Yeshua captivated me when he healed the man at your house, and then he raised you from the dead. You must tell me more."

We heard steps on the stairs and stopped our conversation.

"Well, your patient looks better," Saul said as he stepped off the stairs.

E. Ann McIntyre

"Yes, I was just going to get some soup to see if Boethius can keep it down. He needs some nourishment," Lucanus said.

Lucanus stood up and allowed Saul to get closer to me. He smiled at me, but I sensed there was something bothering him. His pursed lips and crossed arms suggested he wasn't sure about me. The questions started coming.

"Where are you from Boethius?"

"Jerusalem"

"What happened to you that we found you near death on the sea?"

"I was attacked and set upon in Caesarea. Robbers, I suppose. I was knocked out," I said showing him the bump on my head.

"I see," Saul said rubbing his beard.

"What were you doing in Caesarea?"

"I make and sell wine. I was looking for new markets."

Saul was quiet for a few moments. Then he gave me a polite nod and went back upstairs. I was in the lowest deck. The crew quarters and kitchen were up one level. Lucanus went up with him.

Lucanus reappeared with my bowl of soup, which I devoured. He also had a sack with him. I assumed it was his medical bag, but to my surprise, he pulled out a book and a quill. He looked at me and smiled.

"Can we start when you first met Yeshua?"

I swallowed my last spoonful of soup and began to tell my physician the story of my life with Yeshua. He thought the part where Yeshua stayed behind in the Temple and his parents leaving without him was very interesting. Lucanus wrote it all down. He paused me occasionally to ask more questions, especially around our Jewish customs. We spent about two hours together. I enjoyed every minute of it. I was amazed at how much I remembered, especially the things Yeshua said.

Lucanus later excused himself, as he had to attend to the needs of his other patient.

I spent the rest of the day sleeping off and on. Lucanus brought me more soup for supper. He thought it was best for me to have soup for a few days. The bump on my head slowly got smaller under the physician's care.

That evening I shared more about Yeshua with Lucanus. I told him about the Lord's talk on the hillside, and the prayer to the Father that Yeshua taught us. It was late when we stopped for the night.

**

I went to bed that night thanking the Lord for my rescue, and for allowing me to share our story with the physician. All the talk stirred my memories.

We were in the muddy pond surrounded by Roman soldiers. I felt myself smile at the memory dream. I was still smiling when I again felt the Centurion's sword against my neck. Then it started to hurt.

I opened my eyes. There was a sword at my neck. I stopped breathing. In the dim light of the small lamp in my room, I could see a shadow standing over me. I gasped.

"I know who you are, Lazarus of Bethany. I won't kill you now, but you are not coming with us. I will leave you on the first island we come to. You'll die there."

E. Ann McIntyre

Saul of Tarsus left me. I sat up on my bed. I had no idea what I could do. There was nowhere to go. The Lord's enemies wanted me dead.

I remained on the edge of my bed the rest of the night. I could not sleep with the threat of losing my life hanging over me once again. I tried to pray. It seemed just when I needed prayer the most, the words would not come.

I leaned back against the wall. I closed my eyes and tried to remember Yeshua's face. My mind could not form his image. I could only remember him as a boy. The wonder in his eyes when he first saw the Temple. Then, I remembered his raised voice as he cleared the Temple of the moneychangers. I needed him now. I didn't know what I should do. *Should I jump ship? I'd die in the water. I wasn't that great a swimmer. Oh, Lord, help me,* I prayed.

I heard the stairs creak. I sat straight up again. *Had Saul changed his mind? Was he going to kill me now and get it over with?* I was terrified. Then the light caught Lucanus' face.

"Lucanus, you scared the life out of me."

"Sorry, Lazarus. I didn't know if you were awake."

"Saul was here earlier. He knows who I am. He held a sword to my neck. He plans to leave me on an island to die."

"I know. I have convinced him to let you off on an island called Cyprus. He also agreed to let me give you some provisions. I'm so sorry."

"Do you know where this island is?

"Yes, it's off the coast of Asia Minor. I think you'll be all right. Look for a place called Kition. I have a friend there. He too is a physician. His name is

Alexander. All the best, my friend. Oh, and may your God be with you."

I embraced the wonderful physician who was saving my life as best he could. I took the provisions from him. Lucanus waited with me until dawn.

Chapter 33 Thy Will Be Done

"Can you swim?" Saul chuckled as I stared at the expanse of sea between the ship and the shore.

"Saul, you can't do this to him. He'll drown before he gets to the shore. There must be a port nearby where we can let him off," Lucanus pleaded.

"It's up to him to swim to shore if he wants to live."

Saul turned to me, "Now get down that ladder before I cast you off this ship myself."

"Saul…"

"That's enough physician!"

I turned around and put one leg over the side of the boat and then the other. Grabbing the sides of the ladder, I tried not to look down. The rope ladder that had been my lifeline just a couple of days ago was now facilitating my descent to certain death. The Lord's words came to me, I prayed. *Our Father who is in heaven, holy is your name.* I inched downward and struggled to keep the sack of provisions on my back from falling off. *Your Kingdom come, Your will be done on earth as it is in heaven.* I was halfway down. *Forgive our sins as we forgive those who have sinned against us.* I stopped moving. *Forgiveness. I must forgive Saul for doing this to me.* I looked up; I saw only Lucanus' face peering down at me. His hands covered most of it. *Lead us not into temptation, but deliver us from evil.* I took one look down. The sea was calm. *For the kingdom, the power, and the glory are yours, now and forever.* I let go.

I hit the water and sank. I looked up and could see the surface of the sea far above me. I struggled against the weight of the provisions on my back. My chest was ready to burst. I kicked and kicked and finally opened my mouth in the air. I took one mighty gasp and gave thanks. I had made it to the surface.

I looked around and saw that the ship had sailed off. Saul didn't even stay to see if I made it. *Forgive him.* Maybe someday. Right now, I had a more important task - swimming to that distant shore. *James said, "Dogpaddle," Simon Peter said, "Swim like a dog."* I could almost hear their voices.

I still had my provisions on my back. They were heavy, but I needed them. I didn't dare let them go. I didn't seem to be making much headway, the shoreline wasn't getting closer. I figured out that I was drifting sideways more than I was going forward. I needed to swim faster. I picked up my pace, and slowly the shore came closer.

Pushing myself through the water against the current was exhausting. My arms and legs ached. My effort was paying off as the shore seemed within reach. My left hand hit a rock. Then my leg scraped on a rock below the surface. I reached out with both hands and felt with my feet. Solid ground was under me. I tried to stand but my legs, weakened by the sheer effort of getting to shore, would not hold me. As the water got shallower, I inched forward on my hands and knees, small rocks below cut into my flesh. I crawled out of the water and collapsed on the shore. I had made it.

E. Ann McIntyre

I rejoiced in the feel of the warm sun on my back, but I knew I couldn't stay there exposed on the beach. I needed to get up and find shelter for the night. Lifting my head to look around, I spotted a campfire. *A campfire? There must be someone here.*

"Hello, is someone here? I need help!"

There was no response. I dragged myself to my feet. I was shaking as I took tentative steps toward the fire. There appeared to be a small shelter made of sticks beside the blaze. *Maybe someone is in there.*

"Hello, is someone there?"

No response as I finally made it to the campfire site. I sat down and noticed there were two fish cooking on a stone in the fire. It smelled good. My stomach growled.

"I'd recognize that stomach growl anywhere."

Startled, I turned around and saw my dear friend and Lord standing there with a big smile on his face.

"Lord, oh Lord it is so good to see you!" I threw my arms around him. He held me for a few seconds. "James and Peter would have been pleased and proud to see that swimming performance," he said with a laugh.

"I didn't think I could do it, but yes, I heard their words in my head. "Dogpaddle."

"Sit and eat. I have prepared this meal for you."

"Lord, your enemy Saul of Tarsus did this to me. I thought I had been rescued, but he figured out who I was, and put me off the ship hoping I would die. The physician Lucanus was with him. He tried to save me."

"I know. I will have a talk with Saul."

"But Lord, he hates you."

"He doesn't yet know me, but he will."

"Lord…"

"Lazarus do you not remember my words?"

"*Love your enemy. Do good to those who hurt you.*"

"That's right."

"I find that hard to do Lord, but I will try."

"That's all I ask, Lazarus. It will come the more you embrace my way."

We sat by the fire and enjoyed the fish, and some bread from the provisions Lucanus had packed for me. I had many questions to ask the Lord Yeshua, but right now only one seemed to matter.

"Lord, may I ask about my sisters? Are they all right?"

"Yes, they are fine. They are living their mission. They will wait for you."

"So they know I'm alive?"

"It will be made known to them."

The Lord showed me the shelter he had built for me, and told me to get some rest before searching for the town. It was good to know I was not alone on this journey, wherever it was taking me. The Lord told me that my mission in his name was to begin here.

"There are many people waiting to hear my words, and you Lazarus will be the one to take me to them. Through your witness, many will come to believe in me and the one who sent me."

It was late in the afternoon when he departed from me. His visit left me feeling at peace.

***

E. Ann McIntyre

My night in the Lord's shelter was restful. I slept well, only stirring when the sunlight filtered through the sticks. I glanced out the narrow entrance and saw that the fire was still burning.

I got up to see that there were two more fish cooking on the stone. My Lord was taking good care of me. Before eating, I performed the customary oblations and took a moment to pray and enjoy the scenery. The great blue sea had the same gentle waves as yesterday when I swam ashore. The equally blue sky met the sea at the perfect horizon. It was not a scene I saw very often in my life, so I soaked it all in.

The shore I had landed on was actually a small cove. The campsite was in an area of white sand with tufts of grass growing here and there. The rest of the beach consisted of various boulders and rocks. Behind me was a white cliff topped with a grassy plateau.

As I was sizing up my surroundings, it occurred to me that I did not know which way to go to find the village of Kition, which Lucanus had mentioned. I proceeded to do some exploring. Going straight up was out of the question. The cliff that overhung the cove was too steep for me to climb. The only way out of my cove was around.

I checked out the left-hand side of the cove, but a large white rock face jutted out into the water. There didn't seem to be a way around it without going into the sea. So that way was out. It would have to be the right-hand side. There was a rock face there too, but there appeared to be a narrow path around it. I turned back to the cove to collect my few things and to put the fire out.

With my provisions on my back, I navigated around the many boulders and rocks. I took one last look at the sea. There were no ships or boats on the water for as far as I could see. I looked up at the overhanging cliffs. My new life was up there. The narrow path was before me.

E. Ann McIntyre

Chapter 34 Kition, Cyprus

In my estimation, the climb up the path wasn't much easier than climbing up a sheer cliff. I had to kick my sandals off and carry them. My feet were better at digging into the soil. I crawled upward, battering my knees on the rocks as I went.

After several hours of struggling, I finally made it to the top. I didn't even take a moment to look around as I collapsed on the ground.

I laid there until I was breathing normally. Being a priest hadn't exactly prepared me for mountain climbing, so I hoped I didn't have to do that too often. I lifted myself up on my elbows and looked around. There wasn't a town in sight. *Now what*?

Evening was fast approaching and my shelter was far below. The area around me consisted mainly of grassland with a few bushes, not a tree in sight. The slightly worn path appeared to snake along the edge of the plateau. Fortunately, it was only going in one direction.

I struggled to stand and stumbled along the path. It only took a short time for me to spot the town. I was surprised at its size; larger than Bethany, it had a great seaport. Finding one Greek physician would be more of a challenge than I thought.

I found myself wandering from one house to another knocking on doors in my search for the physician Alexander. Soon I would have to turn my attention to finding a place to spend the night. I went down to the port; perhaps there was a place for people who come off ships with nowhere to stay.

I asked a man in an open doorway if he knew of a place where I could stay for the night. To my delight, he invited me to stay with him, introducing himself as Alexander, a physician. When asked, he confirmed that he knew Lucanus. I had found the man I was looking for.

***

My goal over the next few days was to find a Jewish community where I could share my stories about Yeshua. Alexander knew the community well as he was their physician.

The Jewish population of Kition was small, so strangers were not welcomed easily. However, with the good word of a physician they trusted, I quickly became a member of their community. Having been a priest in the Temple also helped.

They were very kind to me. The rabbi helped find me a place to live and supported me until I could find work. I didn't have any working skills besides being a winemaker and vinedresser. Fortunately, an olive orchard owner needed a skilled pruner.

Outside of Israel, the Jewish people lived side by side with the general Gentile community. The Greeks made up the majority of the population in Kition. The other ethnic group was from the mainland of Asia Minor.

The Jewish community was poor, and as such helped each other make ends meet. They had a small synagogue where they met on the Sabbath. I spent a couple of weeks listening and learning about my new community. I received growing acceptance. I waited until the Lord's prompting before I preached about him. The moment came one Sabbath; several weeks after I had joined their community, the rabbi invited me to read and comment on the scripture.

The reading was from Isaiah 61:1. It was the perfect lesson for me to speak to them about Yeshua.

The Spirit of the Sovereign Lord is on me because the Lord has anointed me to proclaim good news to the poor. He has sent me to bind up the broken-hearted, to proclaim freedom for the captives and release from darkness for the prisoners.

"Yeshua of Nazareth fulfilled this prophecy, and I am his witness. I bring his Good News," I proclaimed. I watched the reaction in the room. Twenty men sat in front of me. The women were at the back behind the grate. There were murmurs amongst them. I paused. All eyes were on me. No one blinked. I continued.

"This man Yeshua, healed the sick, cast out devils, and brought the dead back to life." More murmurs and shifting in their seats. I paused again. Some of the men narrowed their eyes at me. I knew what they were thinking. I expected to be kicked out of the synagogue at any moment.

"I am the one he raised from the dead." Gasps came from my listeners.

"I was dead for four days. My body was already decaying when he ordered the stone to be rolled away from my tomb. In the depths of my death, I heard him call me *Lazarus, come out."* I glanced around. Mouths were open in anticipation of my next words.

"Bound with burial cloths from head to toe, I struggled to get out. Yeshua gave another command to those witnessing my return to life; *Unbind him and let him go free*. I stand here before you as a man once dead, now alive, because of the power of God that abides in Yeshua of Nazareth."

The rabbi stood up and declared, "Enough, enough. Get out of here. Do not speak again." He and two older men escorted me out and slammed the door behind me.

***

I sat in my one-room home wondering how I could preach the Lord's word to people who did not want to hear it. I prayed. I remembered how stubborn I, who knew him, had been with the Lord. He was crucified and raised from the dead before I gave him my unconditional belief. I needed to be patient with the people, and be patient with myself.

As I was preparing my supper there was a tap on the door. I opened it and saw two women and a man from the synagogue.

"Shalom Lazarus. We want to hear more of this man Yeshua of Nazareth," the man said.

My ministry began with a few people eager to hear the Lord's words. Within a few weeks, they asked for baptism. More people came, a few at a time. In four months, I had ten people in my community.

Shut out of the synagogue, we gathered in each other's homes. The Lord's spirit was truly with us. We had very few material possessions between us, but we shared what we had. We decided to venture into the community and minister to the neediest people.

The general population started noticing our work. Many people gave us donations so we could distribute them to those who could most benefit from

E. Ann McIntyre

extra clothing, food, and blankets. The more we shared the busier we got. The Lord's vineyard was growing.

Alexander sat in on our meetings. Although he wasn't Jewish, he was eager to hear about the Jewish Messiah who had come to earth as the Son of God. He wanted to be baptized. I told him that according to the instructions I had received from the Apostles he had to become a Jew first. He thought about it. He was fearful, but I assured him that I had circumcised many babies as a priest in the Temple. My assurances didn't help much. As a physician, he knew that the procedure was not an easy one for an adult. He continued to join us for the Word, but I excused him before we celebrated the Lord's Supper. That part, according to the Apostles, was only for full members of the church.

***

Even though our numbers were small, we had much joy in our lives as we shared in the Lord's work. My own job as a pruner was suffering because I was so busy with the church. I decided to invite a couple of others to help me and laid my hands on them just as the Apostle Peter had laid his hands on me. The two men would help me with ministering to the church members, preaching the Word, and taking leadership in the ministries. I also invited two women to serve in the ministry by welcoming new members. They would assist with teaching and performing baptisms.

One of the goals of my ministry was to have a place where people could stay for as long as they needed, no matter their circumstances. A situation near and dear to my heart. Alexander knew why I felt so strongly about creating such a place and offered to help finance the endeavour. I prayed the Lord to bless him.

There were non-Jews who wanted to become full members; a couple of them did, brave but determined souls. Those two men survived my knife. It was much easier for their wives. Alexander still shook his head. I prayed the Lord to bless him anyway.

***

As followers of The Way, we lived our lives in the Lord's love and determination. Although the general population welcomed our service and did not question our beliefs or what God we served, the same could not be said for the Jewish community.

It wasn't enough that they exiled us, but they took it upon themselves to spread untruths about us. Sometimes they would even taunt us, calling us worshippers of a criminal. It was hard for some members who had only recently joined our small church. I marvelled at the strength of the faith of our people. They truly loved the Lord they had never seen. It was humbling.

***

The years passed and the community of faith grew from the inside as well as from the outside. Children came with their parents to our services of the Word and the Lord's Supper. I pondered what to do for those boys in our community who would be

E. Ann McIntyre

turning thirteen in the coming years. We still considered ourselves Jews, so I decided to continue with the Coming of Age celebration. Our members who were Gentiles needed more instruction on the ceremony's meaning and purpose.

The celebration of Passover was something we did differently. While we told the story of the Exodus, we also told the story of the Lord Yeshua's arrest, crucifixion, and resurrection.

The community would not let anyone else tell the story; they wanted me the Lord's friend, and eyewitness, to tell it. When I recalled his trial and death from the stories my sisters and others told me, many people would weep. Others would hum mournful songs. It wasn't until Resurrection Day that I told my story of my friend's resurrection, and how he came to all of his followers in the Upper Room.

After one Resurrection Day celebration, a young girl asked me when she could meet my sisters. She said that I talked about them so much that everyone should meet them.

It occurred to me that I didn't know where Martha and Miriam were. When I first got to the island, the Lord assured me they were well. I missed them. I started to look longingly out to the sea. I often watched ships come into the harbor, and I scanned the disembarking crowd for hours thinking that perhaps someone I knew would get off the ship or even that my sisters would come. Ten years had passed; a long time to experience separation from family and friends back in Judea. I began to wonder if I should go back.

Chapter 35 Visitors

"So, there is a Christian community here. I see you survived the swim."

I turned around to see Saul of Tarsus standing arms folded in the doorway of our dockside shelter. He eyed me up and down.

"Saul please, these people here are poor."

He stepped forward and came within two feet of me; my heart was in my throat. Suddenly, Saul dropped to his knees.

"Brother Lazarus, friend of the Lord, please forgive my transgressions against you."

I was both stunned and perplexed at this act of contrition. I looked up at his three companions still standing in the doorway; my eyes caught a smile on Lucanus' face.

"Saul, I don't understand, what is this about?" I said as I looked down at the contrite man before me. I reached out my hand and helped him to his feet.

"You can call me Paul. I am an Apostle of the Lord Yeshua, your dear friend," he said with a grin on his face.

"How?"

"After we left you in the water we went on to our other destinations. One of those destinations was on horseback to Damascus where, in my zeal for God, I intended to hunt down followers of Yeshua of Nazareth."

I nodded, knowing of his treachery. I was lucky to escape with my life.

"I was just on the outskirts of the city when I was blinded by a great light. My horse bucked and I was thrown to the ground. A voice cried out, "Saul, Saul why do you persecute me?" I asked who he was. He replied that he was Yeshua of Nazareth. I have been his disciple ever since."

I smiled at Paul. The Lord had said on the beach that he was going to have a chat with him. Seems he did.

"Paul, welcome to our humble church. Shalom." I embraced him.

"Shalom Lazarus. Let me introduce you to my travelling companions," he said as he stepped aside and motioned to the others to come in.

"I'd like you to meet Barnabas and Mark. This other fellow you know," he said as he motioned to Lucanus.

I greeted all of them and invited everyone to share a meal with us. I wanted to hear more of Paul's story, and of any news from Jerusalem.

***

Paul made his way around the room greeting and blessing each person. We prayed together before we ate. During the meal, Paul had much more to tell me about the church in Jerusalem and beyond.

"After I encountered the Lord, I went to Damascus and spent some time recovering and learning more about the Lord. I journeyed to Jerusalem to meet with the Apostles. The first time I went, John wasn't there. I think he was unwilling to meet me because I approved the killing of his brother

James. The second time I came he was there. Together Peter, James, the Lord's brother, and John approved of me becoming an apostle and sent me to take the Good News of Christ to the Gentiles. I have been working tirelessly bringing people to Christ and founding churches all over Asia Minor."

"I started the small church here, but don't the Gentiles have to become Jews first?" I asked.

"No, not anymore. Peter made that announcement to the whole church in Jerusalem. Some people disagreed with it but they yielded to the Apostles' decision."

I sat back amazed. I looked over at my friend the Greek physician Alexander. He stared at me with a smile filling his face. I laughed and nodded to him.

"Yes, my friend, yes."

Lucanus reached out and embraced him. "Paul baptized me, almost as soon as Peter made the announcement."

I looked around the room at all the happy faces. By my estimation, the little church in Kition was about to grow exponentially.

Paul had more news for me. "I don't know if you caught what I said when I came in, but those of us who follow Christ are now called Christians, a name first used in Antioch, and accepted by the Apostles."

"I did hear you say that and I was going to ask you what you meant. Interesting, I like it."

I began to wonder what else Paul had to tell me. Not having contact with the Apostles had left me out of many developments, so I was pleased our visitors were here.

"Can I ask something of a personal concern?"

E. Ann McIntyre

"Of course."

"Have you seen my sisters in your travels?"

"Yes, indeed I have. They are living and working in the church in Jerusalem. They went back there after you disappeared. I admitted to them that I was part of a rescue team that plucked you out of the sea. I told them that a few days later, I put you right back in the water off Cyprus and made you swim for your life. Martha was very angry with me. James and Peter had to pull her off me. She said you couldn't swim. Peter calmed her down by telling her that he himself had taught you to swim one summer in Galilee."

Paul looked at me and said, "He obviously did a good job, you made it."

"I did not appreciate having my swimming skills tested in the open sea, but I think you've repented sufficiently."

"Thank you, I do hope you tell Martha that the next time you see her."

"Is there any chance I can get word to them? I would love for them to come and join me."

"I am going back to Jerusalem next week. I intend to go with Peter on his mission to Rome. I can take a note to your sisters if you'd like," Mark said.

"That would be wonderful Mark. Thank you," I said adding, "Peter is going to Rome?"

"Yes, he wants to take the Lord's message to the heart of the Roman Empire. So, I am going as his record keeper, like Lucanus does for Paul," Mark said.

The church was growing everywhere, just as the Lord had said to the first group of believers in the Upper Room. It wasn't without cost. There were still persecutions all over the Empire, but the faith of the people was strong.

"Who will be left in Jerusalem? I asked.

"Peter is leaving the Jerusalem church in the care of James, the brother of the Lord," Mark said.

"What about John?" I asked.

"The political situation continues to deteriorate in Judea. There is a lot of fighting among our people, led by various factions of the Sanhedrin. Everyone is afraid that the Romans will move in and put an end to it. John is caring for the Lord's mother and wants to get her to someplace a little safer. He is considering making a move to Ephesus," Mark replied.

Paul picked up the conversation, "I established a church there. It would be good to have an Apostle of the Lord as its leader to keep the teachings of the Lord and about the Lord within our norms. Some people there are teaching contrary to The Way. I suggested to John that he could go there. As Mark said, he is considering it."

***

Paul asked me if he could preach to my church. I was pleased that he wanted to. Lucanus told me that Paul was an engaging speaker. We arranged for him to proclaim the Word to the community on the Sabbath.

As the day approached, the crowds started gathering outside the shelter, the largest of our buildings, hours before the service was to start. Word had spread that the church was open to all people who wanted to follow the Lord. We had to find another space.

The weather was nice, so we decided to move our service outside. We went to a nearby field at the edge of town. It was a wide-open space that could accommodate a large number of people. I didn't take an exact count, but I'm sure there were over a thousand people in attendance.

Paul preached the Good News, only he used a new term for it, the Gospel of Jesus Christ. He translated Yeshua's name into Greek, which appealed to the majority of the people gathered for the service. I smiled at the idea; *whatever brings people to him, to me he is Yeshua*.

This new Apostle of Christ was a firebrand indeed. I watched the people's faces as Paul expounded on the teachings of our Lord. Eyes were riveted on him, some in tears. So many were deeply touched.

When he finished speaking, he invited people forward to receive baptism. I was amazed as almost every person there came forward. We spent a couple of hours welcoming new members. My little church had suddenly grown from hundred to over a thousand in one day.

Before the end of the service, Paul called me forward. I wasn't sure why. He announced to the community that as the person who established the church in Kition, I was to be its first Epískopos[Bishop]. As the head or leader of the church in Kition, I had the full authority of the Apostles.

He laid his hands on me and declared, "In the name of the Lord Jesus Christ, and on behalf of Peter and the Apostles, I anoint you Lazarus bar Boethius, Epískopos of Kition Cyprus." Then he poured oil over my head. It was a ceremony similar to the installation of the High Priest at the Temple. In fact, to the Jewish members of the church that is what I was. They called me, "High Priest Eleazar bar Boethius." I was indeed following in the footsteps of my father and grandfather, albeit on a slightly different path.

***

After all too brief a visit, the Apostle Paul with his companions Lucanus and Barnabas hired a ship to take them around to the northern part of Cyprus. Paul intended to preach there and found more churches. I bid them farewell and God's blessings upon them. Mark boarded a ship to sail to Palestine and back to Jerusalem. He had my note to my sisters safely tucked in a small pouch. I prayed they would hear my plea and come.

I stood on the dock and watched both ships sail out of sight. I looked back at the shelter that could not hold all of the new Christians. I had work to do, thanks to the Lord's former enemy. *"Love your enemy, do good to those who hurt you."*

"I'm there Lord, finally," I prayed.

E. Ann McIntyre

Chapter 36 Reunion

Over the next several months, I performed the laying on of hands ceremony for six worthy men and women to help me minister to the growing church. Many people came to believe in the Lord and needed baptism. Monetary contributions to our ministry flowed in, so we bought the spot of land where Paul had preached, and started construction on a new place where we could all gather. We still met in each other's homes, where we shared the Gospel and celebrated the Lord's Supper.

Every morning after I said my prayers, I would walk down to the port and watch the ships as they came and went. It had been almost six months since Mark left for Jerusalem. The thought did cross my mind that perhaps he didn't make it. Shipwrecks are a common occurrence on the sea, but I had not given up hope that my sisters would come.

In anticipation that they would make the journey, I bought a larger house that had three bedrooms. With the help of some women from the community, I made it as comfortable as possible for my sisters. I admit I did not know much about how to make a house a home.

One day, I decided to go to the construction site to help with the building of our new gathering place. I was probably more of a hindrance than a help. A number of men in our church were artisans and carpenters, and they would sometimes ask me to hold a piece of wood in place rather than let me cut it. I got the hint.

I watched the men work. To me, it was amazing how plans on a piece of parchment could turn into a building with such precision. I enjoyed watching it happen, and was lost in thought when I heard a voice from behind me.

"Brother, are you ever hard to find."

I turned around, and there stood Martha, Miriam, John, Mariam of Magdala, and Myriam the Lord's mother. I was speechless. I just opened my arms and embraced my sisters. The tears streamed down my face. I only let go when Miriam complained she couldn't breathe.

"I will never let you two out of my sight again," I said. Years of feeling their absence surfaced at that moment. I could barely breathe as I reached out and greeted John and Mariam, and gave the Lord's mother a kiss on her cheek; she patted my face just as my mother used to do.

"I thought you were going to Ephesus?" I said to John after I collected myself.

"We are. The ship will be departing for Ephesus in the morning, so we haven't got long," he said.

"Come to my house. It's not far away."

"We have already been there. We were told you were here." Martha said adding, "I took a look around inside, and you've done a fine job setting it up for us."

"I had help."

"I thought so," Martha said as she gave me a hug.

We all laughed and started the walk back home.

E. Ann McIntyre

***

It was a wonderful supper with joyful talk about the growth of the church, and news from home. They told me about the rising tensions in Jerusalem. John felt it was time to move to a more tolerant place. I told John that we were not welcomed in the Synagogue here.

"That's happening everywhere. We have had to gather on our own. We have to accept that we are now a separate entity from the Jews. A sad thing really, since we are all faithful Jews." John said.

A knock on the door interrupted our conversation. I opened it to see a large crowd gathered outside.

"We heard that there is an Apostle visiting from Jerusalem, and the Lord's mother is here too. We want to see them," a man said.

I turned around and John shook his head, "I'll speak to them later."

I passed on the information and the crowd reluctantly dispersed.

I glanced at Myriam of Nazareth and noticed that she looked pale.

"Mother, do you need a physician?"

"No thank you, Lazarus, I did not take well to being on the ship. I thought I would feel better after I ate something, but I don't. I think if I can lie down on a bed that isn't moving, it might help," she said, with a weary smile.

Martha assisted Myriam to her room where she could get a good night sleep.

John beckoned me aside.

"Myriam is concerned about people knowing she is the Lord's mother. She doesn't want the focus to be on her, but on her son as it should be. It was fine in Jerusalem where she could stay hidden. We need to protect her from the inevitable adoring crowds," he said.

"I understand. We have a shelter down by the port where you can speak to the people if you like; it would take the attention off the house and away from Myriam." I told him.

"Excellent."

***

Eloquence, simple eloquence. That is how I would describe John's words to the people at the shelter. He started with the opening words from Genesis and applied them to the Lord.

"In the Beginning was the Word:
the Word was with God and the Word was God.
He was with God in the beginning.
Through him all things came to be,
Not one thing had its being but through him.
All that came to be had life through him and that
life was the light of men."

I listened in amazement at the profound words coming from the mouth of the Galilean fisherman. John was the first to believe. Before the Lord Yeshua even began his ministry, when the fish jumped into his net, I saw the look of belief on young John's face. John stayed with the Lord all the way to the cross. He even believed that the Lord had risen simply by viewing the empty tomb. It is no wonder the Lord entrusted the care of his mother to his friend and cousin.

E. Ann McIntyre

John continued, *"The Word was made flesh, he lived among us, and we saw his glory, the glory that is his as the only Son of the Father, full of grace and truth."*

When John finished speaking, he went around the room laying his hands on people with physical infirmities. There was a man who was blind - he could see. A woman with a malformed hand - was made whole. The power of the Lord was truly present in his Apostle.

The people pressed in on John, but he backed away. He told them that he was the Lord's messenger, not the Lord.

Afterwards, he explained, "It's not easy bringing the Gospel of the Lord to people. Healing people is only part of the mission. We must take people beyond the physical miracle to the Spirit of the Lord. Belief is hard for some people who are just looking for relief from their problems. The Lord didn't heal everyone who came to him. He healed those who either believed in him already or were on the verge of belief. He knew their hearts. I don't." John said, "I must trust that the Holy Spirit leads me to those who have prepared a place for the Lord in their hearts."

We spent the night in the shelter, leaving the house to the women. John wanted to leave for the ship before sunrise, so they could slip out of town before people came looking for them again.

***

We stood on the dock for a few minutes to bid our friends farewell.

"When will we see you again John?" I asked.

"In the Lord's time. Remember what he promised those of us he called to the roof on the day of his resurrection. He is sending us to generations to come. First alone, and then together. In those days, there will be twelve of us as there were during his time in Galilee and Judea. I have the hair and fingernail samples each person gave me. It is by these things that everyone will know we are Yeshua's friends and the ones he has sent to them."

"How will they know us by our hair? Mine has gone grey since then. Do you need another sample from me?"

"No, I'm sure what I have is what the Lord wants me to have."

"Do you know who the other people are? We were only seven on the roof that night."

"I know of a couple of others, but I'm afraid I'm not at liberty to tell anyone."

"I understand, John. I will continue with my ministry here until the Lord calls me to move on."

We embraced each other. John, Mariam of Magdala, and Myriam the Lord's mother boarded the ship. There were a few people milling around on the dock in the early morning hours, but no one from the church saw them leave.

E. Ann McIntyre

Chapter 37 Valley of the Vineyard

The vineyard stretched for as far as my eyes could see. The work to keep the good grapes growing on these vines seemed enormous. I held my pruning shears in my hand as I took in the sight. I wondered how I could possibly do this work alone.

The dream I had when I was on the skiff at sea became a recurring dream. It was pleasant enough so as not to be a nightmare, but I was truly curious. Where was the vineyard that kept itself in my mind? I wondered if I was just missing my vineyard in Bethany, or if this was something else.

I asked my sisters if they had any recurring dreams about a vineyard.

"I have dreams about the place in Gaul where we were going to go before you were taken," Martha said.

"I have dreams about a strange place, where there are caravans that move on their own," Miriam added.

I laughed, "I'm sorry, but that is funny."

"I know, I'd laugh too, but it seems so real," she said, "I even had a dream about the three of us inside a big carriage with wings that didn't move as we were flying through the air!"

The three of us laughed heartily at that one. My dear sister Miriam had a great imagination.

We were all getting older; maybe our minds were starting to play tricks on us. I had been on

Cyprus for almost thirty years. I had already started to hand much of the work of church leader over to younger men. I felt in my heart that it was time to pick one of them to take over as Epískopos.

***

"It is time Lazarus." I heard a voice in my room. I turned up my lamp. There was no one there.

"It is time to go, Lazarus," the voice said.

"Who's there? Who is speaking to me?" I asked.

"Lazarus – go forth!"

"Lord, is that you?"

"Go to my vineyard. The harvest is plenty, but the laborers are few."

"Where Lord? Where is your vineyard?"

"Come follow me, you and your sisters."

The door to our home flung open. Martha and Miriam were up. They too had heard the Lord's voice. We started to get dressed and pack our things.

"No, take nothing with you. Come as you are, come!"

We left our home once again to follow the Lord wherever he might lead. I could see a being of light moving swiftly along the road to the dock. I couldn't tell if it was the Lord. I couldn't see his face.

When we got to the dock, there was only one ship. Standing on the deck was one who looked like an angel - he beckoned us aboard.

"Who are you?" I asked.

"I am Michael, the Lord's servant," he said, "Be at peace and enjoy the journey ahead, you will be safe."

E. Ann McIntyre

"Are you the one who brought Lazarus home the morning after the Lord was arrested?" Martha asked.

"Yes"

The ship began to move. There were no sails, and from what I could see, there were no oars. The sea was calm. I didn't know how the ship was moving. Michael stayed at the ship's helm. From the position of the stars, we appeared headed in a north-west direction.

We still had our sleeping robes on, as we didn't have time to dress. The early morning on the sea was cool. Michael sensed our discomfort and suggested we go below deck.

The stairway was narrow, I had to turn sideways and duck my head to get below. Once there we saw a table laid out with plenty of food. A fire burned in a small hearth. On either side of the eating area were bedrooms. One for each of us.

Martha ventured into one of the bedrooms on the port side, and found it well stocked with bedding and clothes. Miriam found the same in the other room. I went to the one on the starboard side and was astonished at what I found. There was clothing and bedding as well. There was something else there that caught my attention. I called my sisters over to my room.

Miriam was the first to see it; Martha was close behind her. I pointed.

"Oh Lazarus, it is the model of the Temple that Yeshua made for you during our trip to Nazareth," Miriam said as she embraced me.

"That is so wonderful." Martha chimed in.

"I never expected to see it again. It was too big to take with us when we left Bethany."

I sat on the bed and fingered the exquisite carving. The Lord's attention to detail was beautiful. I had almost forgotten about some of the elements he had put into the model. He carved it when we were twelve, and he had only seen the Temple once. It occurred to me that he had more details in here then he could have known about at the time. I smiled. Of course, he knew every detail of the Temple. It was his Father's house.

***

We settled into our accommodations and enjoyed a wonderful breakfast. As my sisters pondered the nature of our host, I watched the lamp that hung over the table. It wasn't moving. *Curious*, I thought. I sat back in my chair and tried to feel the ship's movement on the sea, but I felt nothing. There should have been some sway, not that I wanted to get sick, but even in a dead calm sea, I should have felt some movement.

I was so lost in my thoughts that I completely missed the conversation between Martha and Miriam.

"What do you think he is Lazarus?" Miriam asked.

"Sorry, who is what?"

"You haven't been listening to a thing we've been saying, have you?"

"Ah no. Who are you talking about?"

"Michael!" they said in unison.

"I don't know. The Lord sent him to take us to where we are going. That's all that matters."

"Well, we think you should find out what he is. Right, Miriam?" Martha said.

E. Ann McIntyre

"Absolutely."

"How am I supposed to do that?"

"Ask him," they said.

I politely excused myself from the table. I had another reason to go topside. I wanted to see if we were moving.

***

I ascended the stairs and Michael greeted me with a nod, "I trust you had an enjoyable breakfast."

"Yes, very enjoyable. Thank you."

"It is the Lord who provides all things."

"Well yes, but you must have prepared it."

"No"

"Then who?"

"The Lord."

I walked towards the bow of the ship.

"I see. Michael, my sisters are wondering about you. They want to know if you are an angel."

"I am a messenger from the Lord. I do the Lord's bidding. I am here to take you to where the Lord wants you to be," Michael said, showing no signs of being annoyed that I had asked again, who he was. He just repeated his same answer.

"I see," I said again as I moved closer to the bow. I looked over the edge. The ship was not breaking water. There was no wake. We were not moving. I continued to walk along the outside of the ship and along the port side. Still no wake. I looked up; we were not under sail.

I glanced over at Michael as he stood by the wheel, occasionally moving it this way or that, seemingly making course corrections. I looked over the edge again no wake. *Interesting,* I thought.

Lazarus of Bethany

As I strolled towards the stern Miriam came up from below. She joined me.

"Well, what did you find out about him? Is he an angel?" she whispered.

"He didn't say. He is a messenger from the Lord. That's all he will tell me."

"Oh dear. How do we know for sure? Maybe he is taking us to our deaths," she fretted.

"I don't think he is taking us anywhere," I said.

"What do you mean?"

"Do you see any wake from the ship's forward movement?"

Miriam peered over the edge and looked at the water. She looked up in the direction where the sails should be, and then back down at the water.

"We aren't moving. Why aren't the sails up?"

"That's what I've been wondering."

"Perhaps you should ask the ship's pilot why we aren't moving," Miriam said with her eyes narrowing.

"I think I will."

I made my way back to Michael. He smiled at me.

"Are you enjoying this lovely day on the sea? I am trying to keep the ship as still as possible for you, so as not to upset sensitive stomachs," he said as he glanced in Miriam's direction.

"Well I'd say you are having great success at keeping the ship still, we don't appear to be moving."

"We are on a journey, I can assure you," he said.

"The sails aren't even up. How can we move without sails or oars?" I questioned.

"We will arrive at our destination at the Lord's appointed time."

E. Ann McIntyre

I gave up and went back to Miriam. Martha appeared on deck and joined us. She looked out over the water leaning on the edge of the ship.

"My, it's lovely out. You can see for miles. Nothing much to see but miles of sea," she said with a laugh. Miriam and I were not smiling.

"What's the matter? You two seem worried," Martha said.

"We aren't moving, yet Michael insists we are on a journey and will arrive at the Lord's appointed time. See for yourself. Look down. Do you see any wake?" I said.

"No, I don't. Are we in any danger?

Just as I was about to answer we were enveloped in a dense fog. We could not even see Michael at the helm.

I took my sisters' hands and held them tightly. "Let us pray." I closed my eyes to invoke the prayer when I heard Miriam speak.

"Lazarus, you better open your eyes."

We were standing on a dock where many people milled around. I looked back at our ship moored nearby. I felt a tap on my shoulder; it was Michael.

"Please come this way," he said as he motioned to a horse and carriage. He assisted Martha and Miriam in boarding the carriage. I climbed in after them. I took note of the baggage. There were three trunks in back, and the model of the Temple secured in place.

Reality was shifting around us like sand around one's feet on a beach. It was difficult to comprehend. I was too dumbfounded to ask where we were or how we got here.

"I am taking you to your new home," Michael said.

I was about to ask where our new home was when I saw a signpost which read, "Provincia, Gaul". I pointed it out to my sisters. Martha was thrilled. Miriam laughed.

Michael guided the horse and carriage inland. We followed a straight Roman road through lush fields dotted with grazing sheep, cattle, and horses. When the road reached the top of a rolling hill, I saw it: the vineyard of my dreams, stretching as far as the eye could see.

"That's your new home," Michael said.

Martha turned around and looked at me. "Lazarus, I think you've died and gone to heaven."

There was a large grey stone house at the edge of the vineyard. It was two stories high with three shuttered windows on each floor. As we drew closer, I could see a barn and another building on the right-hand side next to the house. Behind it were five smaller houses. My sisters sat on the edge of their seats as we drove up to the house.

Michael helped my two wonder-struck sisters out of the carriage. He swung open the double doors of the house. Martha and Miriam practically floated through the entrance. I could hear their "ohs" and "ahs."

As I walked in behind them, I glanced at the other building nearby. I wasn't sure what it was. Michael had my answer, "That is the winery."

I stopped. I think my mouth fell open. It was three times the size of my winery back in Bethany. I promised myself I would explore it later.

I stepped into a large room with chairs and small tables set out as though preparing for people to sit and converse. I followed the women into the next room. It

E. Ann McIntyre

was apparent; Martha had died and gone to heaven too, as she stood in the middle of a very large kitchen. She walked around the room running her hands over the various tabletops, and a large hearth for cooking. On the walls hung every size pot imaginable.

Martha opened a door at the far end of the kitchen. There was a large table, I assumed for eating. There were twelve chairs around the table. Miriam ran across the room and opened a door to the outside. She gasped as she saw a garden of abundant vegetables, fruit trees, and flowers.

"Maybe we have all died and gone to heaven," I said.

"Not quite," Michael said.

"I must leave you now. I have brought you to the place the Lord has prepared for you. Shalom," he said as he gave a slight bow toward us and vanished.

I joined Miriam outside. I laughed as she stood among the roses looking enchanted. Martha was still inside admiring the table.

"I wonder who all the chairs are for?" she said from the inside.

"The Lord said we would be twelve when he called us together again. Maybe we are the first to arrive," I reasoned.

"There were only seven of us on the roof with him that night. I wonder who the other five are. And where is everyone else?" Martha asked.

"I don't know and I don't know," I responded.

"Miriam, would you bring in some flowers for the center of the table?" Martha asked. As ever, Martha did not stay on the same subject very long.

Miriam did as asked. I thought it was time to check out the winery.

As I walked toward the winery, I heard faint voices coming from the five smaller houses down the hill. I stopped and listened. The winery could wait a few minutes.

I made my way down a convenient set of stairs and walked up to the first house. The voices were louder now, and I could hear their words. Whoever those people were, they were speaking in Latin. I paused. *Romans? Maybe they own this place, or they are intruders.*

I started to back up.

"Lazarus?"

I spun around in a defensive style and held up my arms.

"Careful, Lazarus, it's us."

Masters Yosef of Arimathea and Nicodemus were in front of me.

"Shalom my friends, Shalom! I am so glad to see you. We just got here," I said, "I think there are some Romans in that house.

"Shalom, Lazarus," Yosef said as he embraced me, "There are indeed Romans in there. You might like to meet them."

I turned around and saw Pontius Pilate and his wife Claudia Procula standing outside the house.

E. Ann McIntyre

Chapter 38 Forgiveness

"Love your enemies, do good to those who hurt you."

For the second time in my life, I was sitting down to supper with a couple of Romans. Pilate, appearing uneasy, sat directly across from me. Claudia, Martha, and Miriam were happily chatting. Claudia was telling the story of how they came to be here. I could barely look across the table. All I could think was, *"He killed my friend and Lord. What's he doing here?"*

Yosef sat next to Pilate. Nicodemus was next to me. Both men had heard this story before and were sporting knowing smiles. I couldn't smile. *So he went to them after all. Did he have to pick them to be among his new Twelve?* I was not handling this situation very well at all. I wanted to hate the man across the table from me.

Hate is a strong word, but it wasn't exactly love I had in my heart for him. I thought Tiberius had recalled him to Rome and had him executed for treason, after which they threw his body into the Tigris River. Apparently not.

Why are my sisters being so darn nice to him? Offering him pie. I could not tolerate being at the same table as Pontius Pilate any longer. I excused myself and headed for my sanctuary.

***

The winery was dark and I hadn't brought a lamp. I stumbled around hitting my toes against numerous wine vats. I had never been in there before, so I had no idea what was where. I finally sat down to avoid doing any more damage to my toes.

The door was open, and I could see the light coming from the eating area in the house. I was angry. *How long was I going to have to share the same air as Pontius Pilate?* I pondered.

"Lazarus," his voice. I swallowed hard.

"Why are you hiding in the dark?"

I didn't answer.

"Lazarus you are my friend. Pontius is my friend too."

"Lord I can't, I just can't. He killed you. He set his soldiers on innocent men, women, and children. You can't ask me to accept him as one of us."

"Why not?"

"I just told you why not."

"You accepted Paul."

"Yes, but… Lord this is the man who killed you!'

"I know. I have forgiven him. Now, I am asking you to do the same."

"Lord… I…

"Lazarus."

Silence. There was nothing but silence.

"Unless you forgive Pontius Pilate, you can have no part of me or my mission."

There it was - the ultimatum.

I stared out the open door, the light beckoning to me. I had a choice to make. The last time I closed the

E. Ann McIntyre

door on the Lord, I spent a long cold winter on the roof away from my family. The words of the prophet came to me. *Come back to me, with all your heart, don't let fear keep us apart.*

Somewhere inside me, a light flickered. My legs felt a strange courage my mind could not comprehend. I stood up and walked back to the house. Pontius and Claudia were just coming out and going back to their house.

We stared at each other for an awkward moment. Pontius must have sensed my conflict. "Shalom, Lazarus," he said.

"I'm sorry Prefect. I behaved badly, please forgive me," I managed to say.

"It is I who need forgiveness from you and you can call me Pontius."

My hard heart cracked, and I held out my arms to Pontius Pilate. We embraced. A gentle breeze blew around us.

I felt the Lord's touch on my shoulder.

***

I looked out my second-story window at the vineyard below. The vine branches moved in the breeze. I felt at peace, although I wondered why it was so hard to forgive; or maybe I was just a stubborn fool.

A light suddenly filled my room. I knew who was there. He had a smile on his face and held out his arms to me, "Come, my friend. I have something to show you."

We slipped down the stairs and the Lord took me to the edge of the hillside. For a moment, the vines below us glistened as they reflected the full moon above. Suddenly, they vanished. They became people, many people. Some looked bent over as though they carried a great burden.

The scene before me changed. I heard and saw loud banging sounds followed by balls of fire exploding in the air. Fierce warriors ran past us as though we were not there. It was frightening.

"What is this Lord?" I asked.

"These are the times to come when great wars will be fought on this land. You will live to see it. The people you saw will need you. Many of our people will bear the mark of the beast, a number burned into their skin. A great many will die. You, my friend, will survive the horrors of this tribulation. You will take my message to the great generations to come. The harvest is great, but there is much work to be done."

"When will this happen, Lord?"

"When people fail to love, to forgive; when they ignore the plight of the oppressed. It will seem like evil has won."

"What can I do, Lord, to stop this from happening?"

"Love. Work tirelessly in my vineyard. There are many who long to have seen what you have seen, to hear what you have heard. Speak my words with courage, but you must remain hidden as Lazarus of Bethany. The Holy Spirit will guide you and empower all those who I have chosen to remain here until I come. No one will know you are my friends until I make you known at my appointed time. Do not be concerned about the years that will pass. The day will come and you will rejoice."

The Lord vanished from my side. The vineyard was normal again. I realized that it wasn't this

E. Ann McIntyre

vineyard the Lord meant. His vineyard consisted of people, here and beyond.

I knelt on the ground. The task seemed so great. I prayed for strength to carry out the Lord's wishes. I knew my sisters and I would not be alone on this journey, we would have his friends here with us as he promised so many years ago. *"There are those standing here who will not taste death until they see the Son of Man come into his kingdom."*

Amen

I am the vine, you are the branches.
(Jn 15:5)

E. Ann McIntyre

Lazarus of Bethany

About the Author

E. Ann McIntyre

Ms McIntyre published her first ebook of poetry called *'Pages Out of my Heart'* in the spring of 2012. It was followed by a reflective piece called *'An 'Astronomer's Creation Story'*.

Her second novel is "The Feast of Pontius Pilate"

Website: http:\\mcintyreonlinepublishing.ca
Follow on Twitter @mcian157